I0781468

SOMETHING TO TALK ABOUT

Whiskey Mountain Book 1

Samantha Baca

Whiskey Mountain

Whiskey Mountain Series

Something To Talk About
Something To Think About
Something To Believe In
Something To Live For

Copyright © 2022 by Samantha Baca.

All rights reserved. If you are reading this book and did not purchase it, this book has been pirated, and you are stealing. Please delete it from your device and support the author by purchasing a legal copy.

All rights reserved. No part of this book may be reproduced or transmitted in any form or by any means, electronic or mechanical, including photocopying, recording, or by information storage and retrieval system, without written permission of the publisher, except where permitted by law. This book is a work of fiction. Names, places, characters, and incidents are the product of the author's imagination or are used fictitiously.

Cover Design: Richard Baca
Image(s): DepositPhotos

Contents

One
Maggie

"Welcome to Spill The Beans, I'll be right with you," I called over my shoulder as I finished the last few sentences on my recent blog post. I made sure to save the document before I minimized the window and closed my laptop.

My stomach flip-flopped as I headed over to the front counter and recognized the grumpy man waiting impatiently at the cash register. It wasn't his obnoxiously tall, muscular frame that gave him away, nor was it the jet-black hair that was perfectly trimmed and fell neatly into place. It was the piercing green eyes that locked on me and pulled me into the abyss as I stood in front of him. Every single time I looked at him, I could feel myself slipping deeper into their depths.

He looked tired but not tired enough to neglect the thin goatee that dotted his jawline. Apparently, his priorities included grooming and not sleep—not that I was one to judge. I was almost late this morning because I took an extra five minutes to shave my legs even though it was the dead of winter in Montana and no one would see them. But still—it made me feel better.

"Good morning," I greeted in my usual chipper tone. "What can I get you? We have a few specials if you'd like to hear them." I knew that he didn't, but I offered anyway.

He raised a brow and tapped his debit card on the counter. I let out a heavy sigh and pulled my mouth to the side.

"Are you sure I can't convince you to try something new?

Just this once?" I asked, pressing my hands in front of me while giving him the best puppy dog eyes I had.

"No, thank you."

I waited a few seconds to see if he would change his mind, even though I knew he wouldn't. While I didn't know Owen Crawford very well, I knew that he drank his coffee black and shot down every recommendation I had ever suggested to help liven it up.

"Okay," I replied casually. "Anything else this morning?"

"No."

"Not even a muffin? I just baked a fresh batch of *banana nut*," I offered.

I wasn't sure it was possible, but his brows rose even higher on his forehead, disappearing into his hairline.

"Is that supposed to mean something?" he questioned, his voice containing a hint of amusement.

"What?" I asked, looking over my shoulder as I prepared his coffee in a to-go cup.

"The way you said *banana nut*, it felt like there was some hidden message I was supposed to pick up on."

I snapped the lid onto his cup and slid it across the counter to him.

"Oh," I stammered, wiping my now sweaty palms on the front of my jeans. "I just thought, you know, it was a good choice because you're a man."

"And it's a *manly muffin?*"

"Not per se...."

"The other muffins are too feminine for me?" He bent

slightly and looked into the case. "Is the double chocolate chunk muffin not a manly choice?"

"Just forget I said anything," I laughed, waving my hand in the air. I reached forward to take his card as he pulled it away.

The hint of a smile curled up the corners of his plump lips, making my insides feel all mushy. He was staring at me, giving me his undivided attention while I was squirming to get away. Owen NEVER paid this much attention to me, and it was now apparent that my body had no idea how to handle it. I was sweaty and twitchy and pretty sure I might explode from the adrenaline that started pumping through me as I scrambled to talk my way out of this one.

"No way, I want to know what you were insinuating." He smiled. An honest, genuine smile that crinkled the corners of his eyes.

Gosh, he was so good-looking. Older but not too old. Hair that begged to have my hands run through it. Biceps that could easily lift me and toss me over his shoulder as he paraded me down the hallway to my bed.

"I wasn't," I lied, retracting my hand and lowering it to my side while trying to force the inappropriate daydream out of my head. Man, I desperately needed to get laid. But since I was single and Whiskey Mountain was a small town with no prospects, it really meant that I needed a night alone with a bottle of wine and my vibrating rose.

His eyes locked on me, and for a moment, I felt like I was going to get consumed in the thick green forest. *Had I ever seen anyone with such dark green eyes before? They were hypnotizing, and I wanted to get lost.*

"What's so special about the banana nut?" His voice was softer now, all hints of mocking me gone.

I took a deep breath and pulled my shoulders back. He wasn't going to let this go, so I had no choice but to tell him.

"Fine," I sighed. "Bananas contain potassium, magnesium, and B vitamins, which increase the body's overall energy levels. They also contain the bromelain enzyme." I lowered my eyes and looked away.

"And that's supposed to mean what? What does the bromelain enzyme do?"

I felt my neck flame with heat as it rushed to my cheeks. While I had good intentions for recommending it, I never imagined having to explain it out loud. When people came here for a date, I could get by with making my subtle suggestions to the guys, and that was the end of it.

"It helps improve blood flow and increases libido," I rushed out, then tried to cover my last few words with a cough behind my fist.

His brows were back up, drastically high again, as he took in my words.

He licked his lips, and I found myself following the trail of wetness that his tongue left across them. Then he leaned in closer and whispered.

"So, you're telling me that you think that I should have a banana nut muffin this morning because *you're* worried about *my* libido?"

I was suddenly on fire and took a step back. His words shot straight through my body, spreading heat along the way.

"Umm…."

I shook my head, trying to clear the word *libido* from my head. Something about how he said it made it sound so dirty and arousing. *Libido…. Libido… Li… Bi… Do.*

"Maggie?" he asked, pulling me out of my fog.

"Sorry, what?"

He chuckled and tapped his debit card again.

"I was just saying that I'll go ahead and take a muffin," he said, extending his card to me. Before I could grab it, he pulled it back again, our fingers brushing against each other in the process. "Better yet, why don't you make it two."

"Two?" I choked out, finally taking his card.

"Yeah, I wouldn't want my *libido* to suffer this morning."

My heart thumped wildly in my chest as I rang him up, then went to grab his muffins. He thanked me, and for the first time since he'd started coming in two months ago, he smiled at me as he left. TWO smiles in one day? Something was definitely amiss in the universe.

I leaned back against the counter, allowing it to hold me steady as my knees wobbled beneath me.

Men like him didn't exist in Whiskey Mountain, which was why all the women had been going crazy since he arrived. Now I understood what all of the fuss was about.

After I gathered myself again, I went back to the table in the corner that had the best view and started a new blog post. Spill The Beans wasn't just the name of my adorable coffee shop but also the blog I ran that focused on relationship advice. Not that I was an expert of any sort, but if there was anyone who loved love, it was me.

Two
Owen

I sat at my desk, peeling back the wrapper on the muffin. I purposely tried to avoid getting to know people in town since I wasn't planning on staying in Whiskey Mountain very long. Just long enough to do my job, then return home to New York City.

But there was something about Maggie—I finally stopped long enough to read the name tag that was conveniently right above her right breast—that drew me in this morning. Maybe it was that I was too tired to dart in and out of the coffee shop like I normally did, or perhaps it was how flustered she got when she started rambling on about the damn muffins. Then again, maybe I was so used to interacting with people and the constant buzz in NYC that I actually craved talking to someone this morning.

My first meeting of the day had been rescheduled, which gave me the opportunity to google whether or not bananas were supposed to improve male libido. Sure enough, they were a great natural option, and so was pineapple. And after a lengthy search and plenty of rabbit holes later, I also found that if I ate enough pineapple, it would make my cum taste better too. Not that I had anyone to try that out on.

I was single and planned to stay that way. Relationships weren't my thing. Committing to someone who would just turn around and break every promise they'd ever made—as well as your heart—kept me guarded and ready to run the second a woman looked at me a certain way. Trust me—we all knew the look. If you hadn't seen it yourself in person, it was in every chick flick I had ever seen, almost like it was some sort of how-to guide that taught girls how to master it.

I chewed the last bite of muffin and wiped my face with the napkin. No matter how hard I tried, I still couldn't get Maggie out of my head. The way her short hair fell into her eyes when she bashfully looked away, or her full lips that begged to be kissed. She was bite-sized compared to my tall stature, but that didn't stop me from imagining her wrapped around my waist as I showed her that I didn't need a damn muffin to help my libido. Her blue eyes were like kryptonite and had me going crazy.

Once I was done eating, I cleared the trash from my desk and got started with my day. My first meeting this morning was supposed to be with the planning committee to discuss the proposals I had come up with for revitalizing the old, run-down strip mall that sat just within city limits. I knew that I had been chosen for this project because of the recent work that I had done in Fallen Oaks, which was the next small town over.

I had already drafted several proposals that included different options for the committee to discuss. The best option, in my opinion, was for them to knock down the current structure and rebuild. But if I'd learned anything from working in small towns, it was that the locals were rarely ever supportive of destroying an existing establishment and starting over.

There was something refreshing and invigorating about starting fresh and building something new. Being able to make it exactly what you wanted without any restrictions. Not having to worry about what problems might be hiding, waiting to come out like dirty little secrets. That's how I would handle things, but unfortunately, my job entailed that I discuss all of the options available and then figure out which one worked best for everyone involved.

By mid-day, I had rescheduled meetings and set up appointments to look at some additional land that the mayor wanted to discuss. It had been sitting vacant for years, and after I discussed some of the work I had done in Fallen Oaks, we agreed that it might be worth looking into ways to develop the land to create more business for the neighboring towns.

I looked out my office window and smiled at the people walking past, huddling close together to avoid the cold while they rushed into the next shop. It was a small building—roughly the size of my office in New York—with one bathroom, a small room in the back that I was currently using as a conference room for meetings, and the space up front where I'd set up my desk. After working in Fallen Oaks, I knew that it was important to come across as approachable when people came to my office, even if I kept my distance from everyone everywhere else.

This was the second strip mall in Whiskey Mountain, the other one being the property I was supposed to discuss this morning before the meeting was canceled. There were roughly fifteen shops that spanned the length of Main Street. Each one faced the street, and the back of the building was for parking. My office was set up between a cozy-looking book shop and a gift shop that got a lot of traffic. I was also only a few spaces down from Spill The Beans, which I convinced myself was why I stopped by there every morning for my coffee fix. It wasn't that I couldn't just make my own damn coffee—it was as basic as coffee could be.

But Maggie, on the other hand, was anything but basic, and I found myself wanting an excuse to see her more often. My mind knew better than to allow myself to get to know a woman like her, but damn if my body didn't get the same message. The problem was, women like Maggie weren't into no-strings-attached hook-ups, and unfortunately, that's all that I had in me anymore.

Three
Maggie

I sat down at my desk and opened my emails, ready to answer the ones that had come in today while I was working at the coffee shop. Since we were only open until three, it gave me plenty of time to respond to reader emails as part of my weekly *Ask Mags* section, which focused on relationship and love advice.

I sipped my tea and brought my knees up against my chest as I read the first one.

Ask Mags,

I recently found out that my boyfriend has been talking to another woman. He insists that she's just a friend, but I feel like there's more to it. He hides his phone from me, and the other day lied and said he was talking to his mom. I knew he was lying because I had just gotten off the phone with her. What should I do? I don't feel like I can trust him anymore.

-- Confused in Montana

I sucked in a deep breath, cracked my knuckles, and dove in.

Dear Confused in Montana,

I'm sorry to hear that; I can imagine how frustrating and disheartening that must have been to find out. I think there are many things happening here that need to be considered. First, your boyfriend is talking to another woman who he insists is just a friend. If you're unsure whether to believe him, I would sit down and talk to him. If she really is a friend, then maybe the three of you can go do something together so you can get to know her. I understand that he was wrong for not telling you about her, but I think the lines of communication are closed on both ends. Do you think there's a reason he's so closed off and doesn't want to tell you that he's talking to her? Is it possible that he feels you might not be supportive or that you could be jealous of her? I wouldn't jump to the worst conclusion right away, but I do think that you owe it to yourself to have an honest conversation with him. If you're still unsure and unable to trust him, then maybe it's best to re-examine your relationship and see if you can move forward. A relationship without trust isn't healthy and won't last long. Best of luck, and please let me know how it goes.

I pressed send and leaned back against the kitchen chair. While I didn't enjoy these types of emails, I never ignored them because everyone deserved an opportunity to discuss whatever was going on in their lives. And even if this relationship didn't work out for them, I knew in my heart that they were destined to find love. We all were. Some of us just took longer than others....

But, that also didn't mean that my eyes didn't light up and my heart didn't swell when I got the sweet ones about trying to find love, like the next one.

Ask Mags,

Help! I recently started a new job, and my coworker is soooo cute! But every time he tries to talk to me, I clam up and walk away. I can't help it! He makes me shy, and I can't think of anything logical to say. I don't want to mess things up with him by looking like I'm stupid. You have to help me! Show me the way!

--Twitterpated and Confused

I giggled as my fingers began moving swiftly across the keyboard.

Dear Twitterpated and Confused,

This is an excellent thing! I'm so excited for you! But don't worry, those feelings are normal and we've all been there at some point or another.

The next time you see him, try to initiate a conversation. Keep it short and straightforward, and maybe practice saying it in your head ahead of time, that way you don't freeze by trying to come up with something on the spot. It can be as simple as—"hey, it looks cloudy. I wonder if it's going to rain." Once he starts talking, focus on what he says—not what his mouth looks like as he speaks.

Soon, you'll find that the conversation gets easier, and then you can see about asking him out. Start with a casual, easy-going date so you're both comfortable and no one feels the need to impress each other. I always like to suggest coffee dates, and as you probably know—I happen to have the CUTEST coffee shop where you guys can meet! I promise I won't spill the beans, but I'll probably be standing behind the counter, squealing for joy for you! Also, if you do come to the shop, be sure to try the lavender latte. It's a calming mix of lavender, chamomile, and honey—and it's delicious! The perfect combination for those first date jitters.

I answered a few more emails, then shut off my computer. It was early in the day, and I was surprisingly caught up. After the holidays, things usually slowed down for me. Tourists were no longer flocking to Whiskey Mountain to rent a snowy cabin to spend Christmas. Instead, they were all back at home, trying to keep those New Year's resolutions they set a few months ago. Which speaking of, I had started to let slide.

I pulled my hair into a ponytail, struggling with a few pieces that were too short to go in right. I hated my hair too long because it got in my way, but at the same time, I hated it being too short because I was constantly putting it up, which got harder the shorter it was.

The weather app on my phone showed that it was as cold outside as it looked, but that wasn't going to stop me. I was born and raised in Montana, so I was already used to the cold weather. I put on my shoes, grabbed my phone, popped an earbud in my ear, and headed out for a run.

I wasn't one of those people who listened to music while I ran. Nope, I was one of those women who listened to audiobooks and purposely chose the smuttiest one that I could find. Nothing helped me get those extra few steps in like a woman panting heavily in my ear as some devilishly handsome man pushed her over the edge as she climaxed.

My feet pounded the pavement as I sprinted through town, watching out for pedestrians as I breezed past them on the sidewalk. It wasn't my favorite place to run, but the trail I preferred was covered in ice, leaving few choices for me today.

Just as I was about to slow down to avoid an elderly man coming out of a shop, a door swung open and hit me in the face as I ran into it.

"Son of a bitch!" I yelled, bouncing back as I watched the stars dancing in front of my face.

"Oh my God!" a deep voice muttered. "Are you okay?"

I held my fingers to the bridge of my nose, trying to stop the bleeding as I felt the warm liquid drip from my face.

"I'm bleeding," I stammered, unable to lift my head enough to see who was talking to me. Not that I needed to, I would recognize that voice anywhere.

Suddenly he moved, towering over me as his eyes cautiously looked me over, checking for other injuries. His height gave him an advantage so he didn't have to strain to see me, which made me feel ridiculously small.

"What the hell were you doing running here anyways?" he asked, looking around and leading me to the side by my elbow so we were out of the way. He grabbed the travel pack of tissues the old lady handed him before shuffling into the store. He fished a few out and gave them to me. "Is someone trying to hurt you? Were you being followed?"

I sat on the bench outside the bookstore and narrowed my eyes as he kneeled in front of me. I held the tissue tightly to my nose and pinched it. His gray button-up shirt wrapped snuggly around his broad chest, and the rolled-up sleeves showed off tattoos I hadn't seen before.

"Why would someone be trying to hurt me?" I asked dumbly.

"Because you were running like a mad woman down the sidewalk."

He looked at me like it was an obvious answer, then frowned when I let my head fall back and laughed.

"I do not run like a mad woman."

"Normal people don't run down sidewalks."

"There was nowhere else to run." I pulled the tissue away, thankful that it looked like a minor nosebleed that was already starting to slow down.

He continued to study me intently as he stood and folded his arms over his chest. The way he looked right now reminded me of a business casual Superman, and that sent weird tingles between my thighs. Suddenly, I remembered the audiobook that was still playing in my ear. I pulled my phone out, turned it off, and shoved the earbud into my pocket.

He was about to say something but stopped short when the audiobook decided to play through my phone speaker instead of the earbud that I had thought I had turned off.

"Do you like it when I fuck you from behind?" a deep voice asked, followed by a moaning *yes* from a breathy woman. My cheeks flamed with embarrassment as I fumbled with my phone, trying to turn the book off. My fingers were clumsy as they tried to unlock the screen and press the volume button down.

"Take it, Ava," he groaned. "Take this huge coc—"

I stabbed at the screen repeatedly until it finally stopped.

He covered his mouth with his hand and looked away while I refused to make eye contact with him. Nothing, and I mean *NOTHING* this embarrassing had ever happened to me before.

"So, um…" He rubbed his lips together while he continued to look the other way. He shoved his hands into his trouser pockets and rocked back on his heels.

Was this as uncomfortable for him as it was for me?

The way he was now grinning made me think that he somehow enjoyed seeing me embarrassed.

"Do you think he had a banana nut muffin for breakfast?" he asked coolly.

I finally allowed my eyes to lift and found his as they danced with delight.

"Because maybe you were right." He shrugged. "She sure seemed to be a fan either way."

I inhaled slowly and gripped the bench beneath me. This was officially the worst day ever.

"I'm going to go," I blurted out and pushed up to a standing position, only I wasn't quite steady enough to get up that fast after getting hit in the face by a door.

I stumbled and extended my arm to brace myself when I felt his arm wrap around my waist and hold me steady.

"Why don't you come inside for a bit and rest?" he offered.

I looked up, realizing I was standing between the bookstore and his new office.

There was a new sign that had been put up that read *Advantage Realty Group* above the red door. I wasn't sure it was the best color to use for a company that's been proposing tearing down one of Whiskey Mountain's oldest strip malls, but who was I to judge? My door was hot pink with polka dots. Red could also be a color of love, not just aggression.

"I need to get home," I objected, smelling the scent of his cologne as he stood next to me.

"I don't think that's the best idea right now. I'm happy to take you home later when you're ready."

My brows rose with what he said. A few seconds later, he realized the accidental innuendo and cleared his throat.

"I meant I could drive you to your house and drop you off. Make sure you got inside okay without running into any more doors."

"You hit me with one; I didn't run into it."

I let him lead me to the entrance of his office, knowing he was right. I wasn't in any condition to walk home on my own right now.

"In all fairness, I never expected anyone to come flying down the sidewalk like some serial killer was on their heels."

"Are you saying that I run fast?" I asked, looking up at him with a cheeky smile.

"No, I'm saying that you were running like a crazy person. Like Phoebe, from Friends."

"Who?"

He stopped walking and stared at me in disbelief.

"You don't know who Phoebe is?"

"Nope." I pulled my mouth into a thin line and offered a small smile.

"How old are you?" he asked, wincing as he rubbed the back of his neck.

"Twenty-two."

I couldn't hear what he said, but I was pretty sure he had muttered a curse word under his breath.

"Why, how old are you?"

"Too old," he sighed, then went back to leading me inside.

Something changed with him, and his fun, flirty side quickly disappeared and went back to the grumpy, standoffish side I was used to.

"I really should get home," I said, pulling away. "I need to go check on Leroy." I was lying through my teeth—Leroy was fine and didn't need me to rush back, given I had just left him less than an hour ago. But Owen didn't need to know that, and I was desperate for an excuse to escape.

His fingers gripped my elbow again and turned me back toward the door.

"Who is Leroy? I can see if someone else can go check on him, but I really think you need to stay here for a little bit until you can walk right."

My legs felt like Jell-O, but I was willing to run on wobbly legs like Bambi to avoid having to be around grumpy Owen. I firmly believed in people absorbing each other's energy, which meant I tried to hang out with positive, fun people like me and avoid the energies that would bring mine down.

"It's fine; I'll be okay. Thank you, though."

"Maggie, who is Leroy? I can go check on him. Just tell me where to find him, and I'll go real quick."

I smiled and turned to face him.

"He's under my bed. Probably wearing my bra on his head."

He pulled his head back and furrowed his brow.

"Is he your boyfriend?"

I could see the wheels in his head turning as he tried to figure out why a man would be under my bed, wearing my bra as a hat.

"No, but he would make a pretty decent one."

He waited me out and started tapping his foot impatiently.

"He's my pet turtle," I laughed. "Though if I don't get home soon, he'll probably eat my underwear again."

"Do I even want to know?" he asked, rubbing his hand across his strong jaw with a raised brow.

"He can't always see what's food and what's not. Last time he mistook my green lace panties for lettuce and chewed a hole right through the crotc—"

"I get the picture." He held up a hand to stop me from continuing.

"Okay. Why don't I drive you home and make sure you're okay before Leroy eats more of your belongings?"

I wanted to say no. I wanted to convince him that I was fine getting home on my own. I've never needed anyone before, so it was a struggle to admit that I needed someone now.

Before I could object, my knees buckled, and I felt myself in his arms again.

"Okay," I breathed, no longer determined to fight him. "If you're sure you don't mind."

"It would be my pleasure."

His fingers gently trailed down my back before he planted his hand firmly on my lower back and guided me toward his car.

Four
Owen

"Leroy," she called, bending down and looking under the kitchen table as she walked the short distance between the kitchen and living room.

I closed the door behind us, making sure Leroy didn't try to escape.

"Leroy Mitchell Elwood, get your little green butt out here right now."

She picked up a shirt from the arm of the couch and leaned over to look at the floor as she continued to search for the turtle.

I stayed put, not willing to randomly invite myself further into her house to find a lost reptile. My only reason for even being here right now was to make sure she didn't fall and get hurt after getting hit in the face with the door. I still felt terrible about it, but who in their right mind runs down a busy sidewalk with plenty of doors that could swing open?

I heard her voice carry as she went through the rest of the house, calling his name.

As I glanced down to check my watch, a glimpse of something moving caught the corner of my eye and made me jump.

"Son of a bitch!" I exclaimed, moving back as Maggie headed back down the hallway.

She looked at me in surprise before looking down to see what had startled me.

"Leroy," she sighed, walking over and plucking the red lace panties from his head. She quickly pushed them into her pocket and then picked him up. "You know you're not supposed to escape."

I watched as she walked over to a wooden terrarium set up by the floor-to-ceiling window in the kitchen. There wasn't a dining table or chairs, so I assumed she ate most of her meals on the couch and reserved the space for Leroy's cage.

"How did he escape?" I asked, joining her as she sat him down in the terrarium. At first glance, it looked to be in great condition, though when she squatted down to adjust the bottom, I noticed where the two pieces of wood had come apart, and he had pushed his way through.

"He knows that if he pushes hard enough, he can squeeze through this opening. I've been meaning to get a glass one, but I have to find someone to go with me since it's too big for me to bring back on my own without dropping it."

"Have you had Leroy long?"

She shook her head, grabbed a handful of lettuce from the fridge, and then dropped it into his food bowl.

"Only a few weeks. My neighbor got him for her kids, but he scared her daughter, so she asked if I could take him. One look at those beautiful eyes, and I couldn't say no. I'm a sucker." She shrugged and looked adoringly at her turtle. "But unfortunately, her kids were a little rough with the cage, and as you can see, it broke. I haven't had a chance to get a new one, and honestly, he seems to prefer roaming the house anyway."

"Well, if you need help, I'm happy to go with you."

She tilted her head and eyed me curiously.

"Why are you being nice to me?"

I pulled my head back in response. I knew I had never engaged her much in conversation, aside from this morning, but had I been mean to her? I hated the thought that my avoiding people had come across that way.

When I failed to come up with a response to her question, she waved dismissively and started talking again.

"It's okay, I have a friend who should be back in town soon. He has a truck, so I can ask him to drive me over and help me set it up."

I knew I had no right to feel jealous, but I did. And that stupid feeling had my mouth moving faster than my brain could keep up.

"It's not a problem. I can take you now if you want."

"Don't you need to get back to work?"

I glanced at my watch. I still had two hours left and a ton of work I needed to finish before my meetings tomorrow.

"Nope, I'm fine," I lied. "Grab your stuff, and I'll meet you in the car."

Before she could object, I turned and walked out the door, letting out a heavy breath once I was alone.

What the fuck was I thinking?

Ten minutes later, she was climbing in and buckling her seatbelt.

"Where did you want to go?" I asked, starting the engine.

"There's a pet store just outside of town that has the one that I want. But really, we don't have to go if it's out of your way. I can wait."

Her fingers twitched as if ready to unbuckle herself and jump out of the car.

"It's fine, I really don't mind. What's the name of it?"

"Cool Cats. It's my friend's pet shop, and she's kinda—*out there*," she laughed. "I don't know how to explain it, but she's always been obsessed with the prohibition era, so she named her shop Cool Cats, and it's got a speakeasy type of vibe. You can't see into the shop, there's no sign out front, and there's a password to get in."

"You're kidding?" I turned to face her as I headed down the street. That might've been the coolest thing I've heard since arriving in Whiskey Mountain.

"Nope. She loves it, and the people in town enjoy it too. Just something fun and different."

"Sounds like it," I smiled. "I can't wait to check it out."

We drove in silence for a few minutes while she went online to get the password. Apparently, there was a riddle that you had to solve before gaining access to the store webpage. Once you were in, you could place orders online or get the password to visit the store.

"Today's password is All Hail The Tipsy Tail."

I laughed and looked at her.

"Does that mean that there will be drunk cats there, too?"

"Na," she giggled. "Only cool cats and kittens."

I loved how her face lit up with happiness and wondered if she was always this way. I had yet to see her grumpy or in a bad mood, but then again, I hadn't spent much time around her.

"How's your nose feel?" I asked as we headed to Fallen Oaks.

"It's better. I took some Tylenol before we left, but I should have thought to grab an ice pack too. I imagine I'll have a beautiful bruise that I'll have to explain tomorrow. It's a good thing I'm off."

"I'm really sorry," I apologized again. "I feel terrible for hitting you with the door. If I would have known that you were running…."

"It's okay, really. It's not like you could see me. I think your door is the only one on the strip that doesn't have a glass pane."

"I might have to request one now."

"Or I'll just avoid running by your office," she laughed. "Usually, I'm on the trail behind the strip, but it's still covered in ice from the last freeze we had."

The weather hadn't been as bad as I had imagined, though I was also used to winter in New York City. I'm not sure what I was expecting, but something along the lines of extreme blizzards and snow piles that were over four feet tall came to mind.

Soon we were pulling up to an unmarked building with blacked-out windows. I put the car in park and looked over at her with as much seriousness as I could muster.

"If you brought me here to kill me…."

I watched as her lips curled up into a smile as she unbuckled.

"There's only one way to find out."

Five
Maggie

"All hail the tipsy tail," I said into the speaker box outside.

We waited a few seconds, then pulled the door open once we heard the buzz.

I led Owen down the steps toward the entrance, trying not to laugh at how nervous he seemed. If he thought I was going to kill him, I couldn't imagine how he would react once we were inside the store.

His footsteps fell heavily behind mine and stopped as we reached the door. I looked over my shoulder and smiled as I opened the door and stepped aside to let him go first.

"Nope," he shook his head. "Ladies first."

"Are you still worried that I'm trying to kill you?" I laughed and waited for him to go.

"No, but *if* someone wants to kill us, it seems fitting that you should lead the way since this was all your idea.

"We don't kill people," Ramona said as she walked around the corner to greet us. "The wild animals prefer that they're alive so they can hunt them."

Her hazel eyes sparkled with mischief as the parrot on her shoulder squawked *hunt them, kill them.*

"That's enough, Pablo," she scolded, popping a treat into the bird's mouth. "We don't want to scare off our new friend."

I laughed and walked inside, waiting for Owen to join us.

"Ramona, this is Owen. Owen, this is Ramona, and that's Pablo. He has a foul mouth and knows more curse words than a drunk sailor."

"Cocksucker," Pablo squawked and bounced to Ramona's other shoulder. "Pussy eater damn shithead."

"That's enough," Ramona tsked and lifted her finger to transfer him to his cage.

"Sorry," she apologized, extending her hand to Owen. "It's nice to meet you."

"You too." He shook her hand and looked around the store. "I can't believe this is down here; you'd never know from the looks of it outside."

She smiled proudly, letting it stretch across her cheeks.

I excused myself to go look at the new terrariums she mentioned she had when I texted her earlier to let her know that we were on our way. I listened as she told Owen the story about how this building had been in her family for generations and how it once served as a speakeasy during the prohibition.

There were a handful of options to choose from when it came to picking the perfect setup for Leroy. I crouched down and looked over the different bags of substrate to line the bottom of the enclosure. I already picked out a basking lamp as well as a few ceramic heat emitters and made sure to grab a UVB light since it was still too cold to allow Leroy to spend time outside until it warmed up. I grabbed plenty of bags of substrate that was chemical-free topsoil, leaves, and moss and did the math to make sure I had plenty for him to have room to burrow.

It was fun picking out the accessories that would go into his house. Since Leroy was still technically a baby, I read that he needed food at least every 24 hours and made sure to add a plate that would make it easier to eat his food without consuming any of the substrate. In all fairness, he had been wandering aimlessly through my apartment for a few days since I got him and ate holes in my panties, so this was already a step in the right direction.

I was adding the last few things to my cart when I heard Ramona and Owen talking. I leaned up on my tiptoes, trying to hear them better without knocking anything over.

"You haven't read it yet?!" Ramona exclaimed. "You have no idea what you're missing! It's literally the best advice column out there. Maggie *LOVES* love, and it shows every time she writes about it."

"I don't do a lot of reading," Owen replied lightly.

"It's so worth it. Maggie answers reader questions every day in her *Ask Mags* section, but then she also writes blog posts where she reflects on love and relationships. It's so heartwarming, and on occasion, she dives into the good stuff and we get *just the tip*—if you know what I mean…."

"Just the tip," Pablo squawked repeatedly. "Just the tip."

I pressed the palm of my head and closed my eyes. She was not seriously telling Owen about my blog!

Not that I was ashamed of it, but after spending time with Owen, it made me feel a little nervous about what he would say about it.

"She's also known as the town matchmaker. She's helped sooo many people get over their nerves and find their soul mate," she gushed. "It's really amazing. I'm still waiting for her to find her one true love. God knows she deserves it and is holding out for the real thing this time. After what that asshole did to her—"

I jumped away, her words making me want to flee. In the

process, I knocked over a shelf of fish food, drawing their attention to where I was now trying to hide.

"Fucking shit," I muttered quietly. Or so I thought.

"Fucking shit. Fucking shit. Shit on a cracker. Shit on Poly. Poly wants a fucking cracker."

"Everything alright?" Owen asked, rounding the corner and taking in the mess I'd made.

I nodded and scrambled to pick up the boxes as quickly as possible. He bent down and helped, though I could tell his body was way more relaxed than mine. His fingers weren't struggling to hold onto the boxes as he put them back; instead, they gripped each one firmly, and I found myself staring inappropriately.

"You sure you're okay?" he whispered, doing the raised brow thing again.

Why was his cocked eyebrow so sexy?

"Yeah, I wasn't paying attention and bumped the shelf."

Ramona was up front, on the phone with a customer, while Pablo continued with his obscenities.

"What's with the bird?" Owen asked, nodding in his direction.

"He was dropped off with a note that said they couldn't care for him anymore. Ramona took him in but hasn't decided if she's going to keep him for herself or allow someone to adopt him. Obviously, it would take the right people and not a family with kids," I laughed. "For now, they keep each other company, and I think she's gotten used to his random outbursts. The other day, I was talking to her on the phone and heard him tell her to get him a shot of whiskey. Apparently, his previous owner also liked to indulge."

"Sounds like it," Owen laughed, putting the last box on the shelf.

I grabbed the last few things I needed and went up front to pay. I wanted to ask Ramona why she told Owen about the blog but knew I couldn't without sounding weird about it. I've never had a problem with people knowing what I write about until now, but I've also never had to worry about the prospect of dating anyone in town. Until now.

<u>Six</u>
<u>Owen</u>

After I dropped Maggie off and helped her set up Leroy's terrarium, I headed back to the office to finish the work that I needed to get done. While I knew I had a long night ahead of me, I didn't regret spending time with her, which was a bit unnerving to me. The last thing that I needed was to get close to anyone in town—especially Maggie.

I couldn't help but play Ramona's words over and over in my head about how Maggie deserved to find her one true love after what that asshole did to her. Unfortunately, I wasn't given any details about what happened because that was the moment Maggie decided to throw fish food across the store like it was confetti.

I wanted to ask Maggie about it on the way back but knew that it wasn't my place. Not only that, I didn't want to give off the wrong impression and allow her to think that I was interested in getting to know her that well. Granted I wanted to, but there was no way that I could allow myself to act on it, especially now that I knew that Maggie *loved* love.

My computer dinged with another email, forcing me back to reality and away from thoughts of the woman who had been on my mind all damn day. I replied to the email, closed it out, and went back to printing the reports I had asked my friend in Fallen Oaks to send over. I knew there was still a lot of indecisiveness over what to do with the abandoned strip mall, and my goal was to show them the growth that Fallen Oaks was seeing after revitalizing one of their own.

As I stood by the printer and waited, I thought back to being in Maggie's house, searching for Leroy again once we got back. He was probably the best escape artist I had seen and this time was found chewing through another pair of underwear he had stolen from a laundry basket in her bedroom. I had no idea how many pairs of panties she had already gone through, but I had a feeling this turtle was going to be more expensive than she thought at this rate.

Once the pages were printed, I sat down at my desk and stacked them in a pile with the rest of the items I needed for tomorrow morning. I opened a new browser window on my computer and meant to type in *Fallen Oaks Tourism*, but instead found *Spill The Beans* in the search bar as I hit enter.

I promised myself that I would just take a quick glance at the blog Ramona told me about—just to satisfy my curiosity so I could get back to work. But the next thing I knew, it had been over an hour, my coffee was cold, and I was fully invested in *Just The Tip*.

Just The Tip,

My boyfriend has no idea how to make me come during sex. I wanted to bring a toy into the bedroom with us, but he said it was rude and made him feel like he couldn't satisfy me.

Honestly—he can't. But what am I supposed to do? He won't take my advice when I try to tell him what I like, and I can't keep sending him for sugar and flour just to get a few minutes alone with my vibrator. What do I do?

-- Buzzing and Frustrated

Dear Buzzing and Frustrated,

I can imagine just how frustrating that is. I think you deserve to get what you want out of your relationship, and that means in the bedroom. Have you thought about going to one of those Deliciously Pink parties? They have ones for couples, and a trained professional talks about different toy options and how to use them as a couple. He may not know that toys can be just as fun for him as they are for you. I would sit down and talk to him first, but if he's still not interested, then maybe it's time to consider whether you'll be satisfied by staying in this relationship.

One of the most essential components of any relationship is being able to feel loved and trusting your partner. If you can't openly discuss what you want with him, he may not be the one. Hopefully, he'll take a step back and listen to what you're asking for. Just make sure to do it at the right time— as in not in the bedroom, during sex, or before you think you might have sex. He's going to be more likely to shut down and not hear what you're saying during these times.

And, if all else fails, send him over to Spill The Beans to grab you a lavender latte while you get your buzz on! There's no shame in bringing toys into the bedroom; always remember that.

I swallowed hard and adjusted the tie that suddenly felt too tight around my neck. This was a different side to Maggie that I honestly hadn't expected to see. I tried to force myself to close the window and get to work, but once again, I found myself clicking on the next one.

Just The Tip,

I had a sex dream last night, and it's FREAKING me out.

It's not just the fact that it wasn't about my boyfriend, but that it was HIS DAD instead. I could feel everything he did to me in my dream as he pounded into me and made me come multiple times. It was an amazing dream, and I was so disappointed when I woke up.

But that's not the only problem. Not only do I feel guilty about fantasizing about my boyfriend's dad, but I'm also embarrassed that I'm disappointed that he got me off so well in a dream, yet his son can't give me an orgasm to save his life.

What do I do? I can't pretend that the dream didn't happen—nor do I want to! But I also can't just break up with my current boyfriend and go ask his dad to rail me. Am I a horrible person?

-- Dream Slut

Dear Dream Slut,

Can I just start by saying I don't love this name for you? Fantasizing about someone in your dreams is an action by your subconscious and is no different than having a dream about going off and murdering a bunch of people because they ate the last donut. You wouldn't wake up and continue to obsess over such a random—and made-up—act of violence, now would you? Though, I would personally probably still obsess over the donuts because, well, donuts.

But that's not what you asked for my help with, so I'll get to the point. You're not a slut for dreaming of your boyfriend's dad. Our brains are tricky, and who knows why your subconscious chose him to put into the sex dream, but it sounds like it was an amazing one. Maybe you had recently interacted with him, or something reminded you of him, and that's why he popped up in dreamland. Either way, it doesn't sound like you're usually sitting around obsessing over dirty thoughts with him, so I wouldn't put too much concern into it.

Now, onto the bigger issue. You've said that you woke up feeling frustrated that your boyfriend doesn't get you off. That's a problem that a lot of women face—and men, if you're reading this—LISTEN UP.

It takes a lot more to get a woman to climax than it does for men. It's not as simple as just stroking a cock for a few minutes to get the job done. Our bodies are made differently, and our minds play a huge role in whether or not we're able to get to the big O.

Sometimes we're in the mood and can get there relatively quickly with direct pressure on our clit. Other times, we're too busy making a to-do list for the weekend or trying to remember what items we need to add to our grocery list. It isn't that we don't want it; we just sometimes struggle to get out of our heads.

I recommend discussing this with your boyfriend and seeing what changes you guys can make. Does he try to get you off? Is he using a touch that you enjoy? Maybe you can try having him talk dirty to you if you're not able to get your head clear while he's touching you. Or even better, maybe show him what you like and touch yourself while he watches. It can be incredibly arousing to watch your partner masturbate.

If those things don't work and you're still obsessing over his father, maybe ask him if he thinks his dad would be interested in a threesome. Totally kidding—unless you think he'd be into it—then I say go for it.

Keep me posted, dream slut.

I didn't know that it was possible to feel so aroused by reading Maggie answer sex questions in a damn blog, but the way my trousers were suddenly snug against my cock proved that it was. Frustrated, I pushed my chair away and took a trip to the bathroom.

<u>Seven</u>
Maggie

"How is Leroy adjusting to his new home?" Ramona asked as I pushed my phone between my ear and neck to hold it in place while I loaded clothes into the washer.

"He seems to like it," I said, looking over my shoulder to see him trying to ram it open with no luck. "Though I think he much prefers to be out roaming my apartment and eating my underwear."

"How many pairs has he devoured?" She laughed, and I knew she thoroughly enjoyed hearing the stories of Leroy and his crazy antics from the moment I adopted him.

"Seven," I sighed. I tossed in the last few garments and closed the lid.

"How did he get ahold of that many? Do you just have underwear lying all over your house?"

"No. I recently went shopping and bought all new underwear after my breakup with Samuel. It was my gift to myself for walking away from such a toxic relationship. I just got them on Sunday, then Liz brought Leroy over that night, and everything has been hectic and chaotic ever since. I didn't have a chance to pick the bag up off the floor by my dresser, and he's been sneaking in and stealing them. Every time I finally remember, something else happens, and I get distracted."

Ramona laughed louder, encouraging a loud squawking laugh from Pablo.

"It's not funny," I whined. "By Wednesday, I finally remembered and picked them up off the floor. But then I put them in the hamper, and he found a way to pull them through the holes to get them out. He's obsessed."

"Is it just panties?"

"Pretty much, though I did catch him wearing one of my new bras on his head the other day. But I think it fell on his head when he was rummaging through the bag, trying to get to the good stuff."

"I've never seen an animal so obsessed with eating clothes than Leroy. I wonder why?"

"Probably because he knows how expensive they were. My name isn't Victoria, and it's no secret that I over-indulged in buying more than I needed. I even bought a few new pieces of sexy lingerie, though Lord knows I'll only be wearing them for myself."

"Don't say that." Her voice softened, and I could tell that mentioning my pending doom of singledom had dampened the conversation.

"It's true." I sat down on the couch and pulled off the lid of the Ben and Jerry's pint I had opened last night. "My only true love is Chunky Monkey because that's what I'm going to be if I don't stop eating ice cream for dinner every night."

"You're not chunky, though I think you're onto something with the monkey and bananas." She laughed, and I knew what she was getting at.

"You read my recent blog post," I giggled, lifting the spoon to my lips and allowing the cold metal to sting for a second before taking a bite.

"I sure did. Who knew that there were that many foods that could have sexual benefits? I swear, I'm going to start eating better."

"Why? It's not like you and Daniel don't have a great sex life. God knows I hear about it often enough."

"Dan's the man. Dan's the man. Do it alllll nigghhttt. Dan's the big man."

I choked on the next spoonful of ice cream as I tried to hold in my laughter at Pablo's outburst.

"Dan give it to you how you like it. Dan has a big coc—"

"Okay, that's enough out of you, bird," Ramona mumbled something else before I heard the metal cage shut and shuffling on the other line. "Sorry, he overhears way too much."

"So, Dan's the man?" I smiled cheekily, taking another bite.

"Most of the time. But that doesn't mean that I skip over *Just The Tip*. I don't know what makes you more popular in town, your incredibly sweet blog posts about love and romance, or the down and dirty details you get into in the *hidden* part of the column."

"It's not so hidden if people can find it."

Sometimes I hated that it was so easy for them to locate it. Just a few clicks on the menu, and they'd find the ominous link at the bottom. I should have taken Ramona's lead and gone with a speakeasy vibe that required a password to access it. Oh well, it was too late to worry about that now.

"Apparently so is the g-spot, not like I would know."

"Still no luck with that?"

"Nope. And I asked Dan about going to one of those classes with the sex toys, but he immediately rejected the idea. I think he thinks we're fine because I have an occasional orgasm, but I'm not gonna lie—sometimes I want to punch him in the balls when he comes and I don't."

I pressed my lips together to keep from laughing.

"Okay," she sighed. "I know. I'm being dramatic. It's every time."

I tipped my head back and let it out. She quickly joined in, and I remembered why having a rowdy best friend was the best therapy I could have.

"Well, it's not like I would know what they're like either," I said quietly, depositing the empty container into the trash before adding *Chunky Monkey* to my shopping list on the fridge.

"It'll happen soon enough. Don't stress about it."

"I'm twenty-two, Ramona. Twenty. Two."

"Relax, it's not like you're turning forty and still a virgin," she laughed. "You're still young; you just haven't met the right guy to share that with."

"The older I get, the harder it will be to find someone willing to take it. I'm going to have to be like one of those homeless people on the corner with a sign begging for money. But instead, it's going to be me begging them to take my virginity."

"That's not going to happen."

"It could."

"If you stood outside with a sign advertising that you wanted to have sex, you'd have all of Whiskey Mountain lined up, as well as all of Montana. Trust me—guys have no problem taking a girl up on her offer to have sex."

"I know," I exhaled slowly. "That's not the problem, and we both know it."

"Yeah, we do. It's not just having sex that you want. It's finding someone worthy of earning it from you. Someone who you're in love with."

We sat quietly for a few minutes, letting the words float in the air around us.

"See, it's never going to happen. I can help others work through their problems and find their happily ever afters, but I can't even find a nice guy worth dating myself. It's hopeless."

"It's not hopeless."

I felt my shoulders tense and hated that I was now out of ice cream. It was too late to run out and get some now. Everything in town had closed an hour ago, and I wasn't willing to drive a few hours out of the way for it. At least I was off tomorrow, so I could lay in bed and wallow in self-pity for a bit before forcing myself to get up and go for a run.

My fingers reached up and gingerly touched the bruise on my nose. Maybe I wouldn't run through the strip mall tomorrow. But then again, maybe I could run into Owen. Not literally, of course; that was a little painful.

My mind had drifted to thoughts of him and our afternoon spent working on putting the terrarium together for Leroy. He had even been kind enough to stop by the market so I could grab a few groceries before he dropped me off. It had been nice to see him laughing and more relaxed than he usually was when he came in for his daily black coffee. When I first met him, I thought he was just some arrogant ass from NYC and couldn't wait for him to leave town. But now, I was second-guessing my opinion of him. I couldn't help but wonder who Owen really was and if I'd get another chance to get to know him.

Eight
Owen

The next few days were busy, but thankfully the meetings had gone smoothly. I had met with the mayor, the city council, and the planning committee to discuss the options for the current strip mall that I had been brought in for, as well as a few vacant pieces of land that Mayor Landing inquired about.

Saturday morning, I got up early and headed out to run a handful of errands. Besides grocery shopping, I desperately needed to wash my truck to get the mud splatters off from the recent storm. Usually, I made coffee at home on the weekend, but since I was officially out of that, I found myself walking into Spill The Beans as my nerves balled in my stomach.

There were a few people in line, so I took the opportunity to stand back and watch Maggie as she worked. Her brown hair was pulled into a ponytail that bounced lightly as she moved around behind the counter, working on orders. You could tell that she knew the locals because of how her blue eyes crinkled when she laughed at something they said.

I hated the way I felt drawn to her, constantly pulled into this world that I didn't belong in. I knew she was younger than me—though I didn't realize how young until a few days ago. Twelve years might not be a big deal to some people, but in my head, it was a huge fucking deal when it meant that a thirty-four-year-old was hitting on someone who was barely legal.

The line moved forward and her eyes lit up when she saw me. She gave me a small smile before tucking a strand of hair behind her ear that had fallen out of her ponytail. I could tell she was just as nervous to see me as I was to see her, though I didn't know why.

For me, I needed to make sure that when I talked to her, I did it with my head on straight and not with my dick. The last thing I wanted to do was lead her to think that I was interested in getting to know her, even if it made something deep inside me ache at the thought of never knowing who she really was.

I had spent the past few days convincing myself that I was simply infatuated with her because she was like a shiny new toy, and I wanted to play with it. Okay—her—I wanted to play with her.

Which was exactly why I should have avoided coming here this morning. There was a café just a few blocks away that served coffee that I could have gone to instead. Hell, I went there every now and then when I needed a caffeine fix and Spill The Beans was closed. But for whatever reason, I was stupid enough to convince myself to come here and believed that seeing her wouldn't have any impact on me.

My heart started racing, and before I knew it, I was next in line.

"You ready?" she asked, leaning forward over the counter as if she was calling over a scared puppy that was stranded on a busy highway with cars darting toward it.

"Yeah," I cleared my throat. "Sorry."

"No worries." She laughed, but it didn't meet her eyes the way it did a few minutes ago when she was talking to the older couple and promised to come by to try the huckleberry jam their daughter had made. "What can I get you?"

I could tell she was used to asking everyone because she shook her head and entered something into the computer.

"Sorry," she laughed again. "Coffee black." She looked up, and our eyes locked. "Anything else?"

"I um," I cleared my throat again, hating that it was suddenly so dry. "Actually, I thought I would try something new this morning."

What the hell? I didn't drink fancy coffee. What was I planning to order? I was going to sound like a dumbass for asking for something like—coffee with sugar, please. Look at me—could I be any more adventurous?

"Yeah?" She tilted her head and looked genuinely surprised.

I nodded but kept my mouth shut.

Don't look stupid. Don't look stupid.

"Okay," she spoke slowly, again like she was approaching a skittish dog. "Did you have something in mind?"

I opened my mouth to tell her never mind, and I would just do my usual, but snapped it shut.

"I thought maybe you might have a recommendation for me?"

Her eyes widened, showing me the most beautiful blue I had ever seen. The ocean had nothing on the radiant color looking at me.

"Is there anything you *don't* like? Honey? Cinnamon?"

I looked behind me, nervous that I was holding up the line but felt oddly comforted that there was no one behind me.

"I have no idea," I laughed nervously. "As you know, I don't experiment much with my drinks."

She laughed and reached across the counter to gently squeeze my hand.

"Don't worry; I think I have something you'll like."

She let go, and I immediately missed the warmth of her soft skin. I knew that I shouldn't, but I was also human, and it had been a long time since anyone had touched me aside from the men who shook my hand in the meetings yesterday. Oddly enough, the women already felt like we were "family" and insisted on hugging instead.

I stepped to the side and watched as she worked. She'd look over her shoulder every now and then, probably checking to make sure I hadn't darted out of the shop and changed my mind.

Whatever she was making smelled delicious, which was a good thing, given that I had already decided to commit to this stupid idea.

A few minutes later, I watched as she snapped a lid on a to-go cup and slid one of those protective sleeves on.

"Here you go," she said, extending it to me. "It's a flat white, which is simply espresso with steamed milk on top. Nothing too sweet or complicated."

She smiled proudly and watched as I took a sip.

I closed my eyes as the hot liquid touched my lips then moved on to grace my tastebuds.

She was right all along—this was delicious. Why hadn't I given in to allow her to make any suggestions before now?

Maybe I had just been too busy, or maybe it was because small-town women were different from the women in NYC. Back home, no one bothered to make recommendations or took the time to ask what you liked. You got in, ordered your drink, and got out of the way because there was a line a mile long and wrapped around the building. I had told myself the moment my plane landed in Montana that I needed to remember that people, in general, were different here, and Maggie was proving that right now.

"So," she asked nervously, watching me as I took another

sip. "What do you think?"

"It's delicious," I admitted and lowered the cup from my mouth so she could hear me. "Thank you."

She giggled and looked away, but not before I noticed a slight blush creep up her neck and onto her cheeks.

I narrowed my eyes suspiciously, wondering if she was now making fun of me for my drink choice.

"Sorry," she laughed more and then pointed to my mouth. "You have a little foam mustache, and I can't stop staring at it. It's so cute that I just want to reach over and…."

Her words stopped suddenly, and while I was thankful that she hadn't continued her sentence, I also hated not knowing what it was. *Reach over and wipe it off with her fingers? Reach over and lick it off with her tongue? What did she want to do?*

"Thanks for telling me," I said with a chuckle and then wiped it away. "See, this is why I stick to black coffee." I winked to let her know that I was joking but then regretted it because it also felt like maybe I was flirting with her. And by the way her cheeks flushed even more, I knew she was thinking the same thing—I was flirting with her.

"How much do I owe you?" I asked abruptly, causing her to flinch slightly. I pulled my wallet out and kept my eyes on finding my debit card to avoid looking at her.

"Don't worry about it," she said quickly, putting her hand out to stop me. "It's on the house."

"No, really, I insist on paying."

"Thank you, but I refuse your payment. You finally gave in and allowed me to recommend something new, so it's my treat."

I knew how she was looking at me, even without lifting my eyes to see it. I could feel it in my body, and with any other woman, it would have been a clear sign for me to invite her back to my place. But this was Maggie. Twenty-two-year-old Maggie. Small-town Maggie who wanted to find true love. I didn't have to ask to know that she wasn't also no-strings-attached Maggie, which was why I tucked my wallet back into my pocket, muttered a quick thank you, and got the hell out of there.

Nine
Maggie

I woke up Sunday morning feeling tired and achy. I had tried to get a good night's sleep last night, but I was restless and had terrible dreams that Leroy had escaped his new home and ate my entire house. For some reason, it was believable enough that I got out of bed around 4:30 to make sure he hadn't devoured the living room like I had seen in my dream. After that, it took forever to fall asleep, leaving me feeling slightly grumpy this morning. Good thing it was Sunday, and Spill The Beans was closed today.

After making a quick stop in the bathroom, I padded down the hallway, rubbing the sleep from my eyes so I could see to start the coffee. Today was supposed to be my self-care day, which meant that I wasn't likely to change out of my flannel pajamas or comb my hair. Or at least that's what I told myself when I needed an excuse not to do it.

I loaded the Keurig and pressed start, anxious for that first drop of sweetness to hit my tongue. I loved coffee more than anyone I knew, which meant I treated myself to the good stuff at home.

While the sweet aroma filled the kitchen, I grabbed my laptop and sat on the couch. Running Spill The Beans was probably my favorite part of my life, and it never felt like a chore to read the emails that came in with people asking for advice. I glanced over at Leroy as he paced around his terrarium and wondered whether that was still true. Now that I had him, he might very well be my favorite thing.

I logged into my email and waited for the page to load with the new messages while I got up and fixed my coffee. I heard the distinctive ding as the emails came through and decided to make a quick bagel while I was up. Once I was done, I curled up on the couch and got settled. I pulled the TV tray close to me and opened the first email.

Ask Mags,

I'm not sure why I'm even writing to you, but I guess that's what a few fingers of whiskey does to some people. I know that I don't need help, but I'm also not sure what to do.

I like a woman that I just met, and I find myself feeling drawn to her in a way that I've never experienced with anyone else. The problem is that she's looking for a serious commitment, and I'm not a relationship or commitment type of guy. We're as opposite as opposite can be.

No matter how hard I try, I can't get her off my mind. How do I get over someone I was never supposed to allow myself to get attached to in the first place?

--Stupid In Montana

I took a sip of coffee and held the warm mug between my hands as I reread the email. There was something about the email that kept sending a dagger straight to my heart, but I couldn't figure out why.

I went to the next few emails and tried to focus on them, but it was pointless. My mind was still focused on the first one, and I knew that I couldn't move on until I'd at least tried to answer it. Only, I didn't know how to answer it because it sounded like they already knew that they didn't want to get involved with this person for whatever reason.

Dear Stupid In Montana,

You don't sound stupid to me. In fact, you sound like you know exactly what you want, even if you're struggling to allow yourself to have it. I know that you said this woman is looking for a serious commitment, and that's not something you're interested in. Still, I'm curious to know if you've had this conversation with her or if you're assuming that's what she's interested in.

I know a lot of people who have a general idea of what they want out of life, but that doesn't mean that they might want different things along the way. Take me, for example. When I was younger, I was convinced that I would be married and starting a family by the time I was twenty-three. Given that I'm single and already twenty-two, I'm going to say that I don't think this is a realistic goal after all. Does that mean that I've given up all hope for ever having the family that I want to have? No. It just means that my future looks different than I thought it did when I was younger.

Just because I want to be married and have a family someday doesn't mean that I would rule out dating anyone right now if they didn't share the same vision as me. Who knows what can change along the way, and more importantly, imagine what would happen if I missed out on meeting the person I was meant to be with by limiting myself so early on.

I don't know the reason why you're against commitment or being in a relationship, but I would like to encourage you to step back and consider whether those things are still as important to you as they once were. If not, maybe it's worth exploring what could be there with this woman you can't stop thinking about. Just saying that's how a lot of the great love stories start…

I pressed send and moved on to the next few emails while I ate my bagel. The morning was already starting to feel better now that I'd had some coffee and was doing what I loved most—helping others find love. I had just finished replying to all of the new emails when another one popped up in my inbox.

Ask Mags,

Unfortunately, I don't think it's that simple. See, I've been in committed relationships in the past and have seen firsthand how quickly you can get hurt. I've put myself out there, taken the steps to move forward, and was left at the alter as my bride-to-be ran off with the best man—aka my best friend.

This woman, she's light in the darkness. She's the good in a world filled with evil. She's everything I'm not and deserves better than I could ever give her.

I'm not destined for great love, and I wouldn't want her to miss out on hers by wasting her time on me.

--Stupid In Montana

My heart sank as I read the words on the screen. He had written back, which meant he was likely sitting somewhere, waiting for my reply.

This time, I decided to reply privately to him and not through the blog. He seemed like someone who could use a friend, and I didn't want him to stop talking to me if he thought I would publish all of it on the blog.

My fingers moved quickly across the keyboard, eager to reply.

It's Okay To Be Loved In Montana,

I took the liberty of changing your name for you. You're welcome (winking emoji). There's nothing stupid about your situation, and thank you for sharing some more of your story with me.

I understand how guarded you must feel after having your fiancé leave you on your wedding day with your best friend. I can't imagine the heartache that must have caused you. I hope you at least had the opportunity to indulge in some cake and drink the champagne. That sounds like how I would have handled it if it was me!

Going through a breakup like that would leave anyone guarded. I can empathize with why you don't want to get involved in another committed relationship, but I think you also owe it to yourself to try.

You're not someone who doesn't want love, you're someone who doesn't want to get hurt. And if you put yourself out there again, there's a chance it could happen. The only way to keep from feeling that pain again is to close yourself off and not allow anyone to get close to you.

I totally get the thought process and the desire to protect yourself, but I also want to remind you that not all women are like your ex. In fact, very few of them are.

If you're feeling chemistry with this other woman, I think you owe it to yourself to explore what those feelings are. You don't have to rush into anything. Take your time. Be honest with her, as well as with yourself. If it doesn't work out, then at least you can say that you tried. It's better to at least take a chance and know what it is than to be too afraid to go for it and constantly wonder what could have been.

I sighed heavily, pressed send, and then waited for a response that never came.

56

Ten
Owen

I continued staring at my laptop, reading the response that I had gotten back from Maggie this morning. I hadn't imagined that she would reply to my email, but then again, I hadn't meant to send one to begin with.

Last night had been rough, and I had handled it the best way I knew how at the time—whiskey.

Between seeing Maggie at Spill The Beans yesterday, then getting a call from Sebastian—my former best friend—I was feeling a little more than slightly off-kilter. It wasn't the first time he'd tried to call me in the fourteen months since he'd run off with my fiancé on my wedding day. But it was the first time I had listened to the voicemail he left after I'd refused to answer.

"Owen, please call me. I want to explain what happened. We didn't mean to hurt you. It wasn't supposed to happen this way."

I pressed delete before he could continue and then blocked the new number he had called me from. I was usually a rather forgiving person, but even I had boundaries, and they both had crossed them.

When I'd emailed Spill The Beans blog, I assumed it would be lost in the depths of darkness on the internet or sent to the spam filter. Never in a million years did I think that Maggie would think my pathetic email was worth responding to. Which just went to show what kind of person she really was.

You're not someone who doesn't want love, you're someone who doesn't want to get hurt. And if you put yourself out there again, there's a chance it could happen. The only way to keep from feeling that pain again is to close yourself off and not allow anyone to get close to you.

Her words had sent an anchor right through my heart and wedged itself there. She was spot on, as always. Just like her, I'd once had the same dream of one day having a family and the happily ever after, but I'd been jaded ever since Brittany walked out on me. She was supposed to be the love of my life, the one I'd chosen to be my forever. Aside from the anger I felt from her betrayal, I'd also harbored a large amount of bitterness with myself for not seeing before then that she didn't love me the same way I loved her. That might have been what hurt the most—that I was so blinded by the idea of having what I thought I always wanted that I didn't actually see what was in front of me.

I totally get the thought process and the desire to protect yourself, but I also want to remind you that not all women are like your ex. In fact, very few of them are.

I knew that Maggie was right; not all women were the same as Brittany. But that didn't help me let my guard down any when it came to thoughts about Maggie. Even if she didn't want a committed relationship right now—despite what Ramona told me when Maggie wasn't around—that didn't mean that she was someone I should try to start something with.

For one, she was much too young for me. Twelve years to be exact. Maybe it wouldn't be such a big deal if she was older, but she was still technically a kid as far as knowing what she wanted out of life.

By that afternoon, I had considered replying to her email but didn't know what to say. Everything that I typed out was just as quickly deleted. I didn't want to acknowledge that she was right because once I allowed that thought to fester in my head, I knew that it would be even harder to keep my distance from her.

So instead, I changed clothes and went for a quick run, making sure to avoid any pedestrians on Main Street.

The cold air felt good against my face as I pushed myself to run faster. If I could burn off some of this energy, then I would be in a better head space the next time I went into Spill The Beans. Granted, I could just stop going there, but to be completely honest, the coffee wasn't nearly as good at the café. Maggie had really done me in yesterday with the concoction that she made me, and now I knew that I wouldn't be as content with plain black coffee anymore.

It wasn't that it was Maggie's fault—though technically it was— but it was almost like she had some sort of magic and kept me locked under a spell. A deliciously flavored coffee spell.

I turned the corner, allowing my body to slow for a brief moment as I kept along the side of the mountain. It wasn't that high up the hill but was one of the few trails I had found that didn't have a thick layer of ice. Even though I still stood by my statement that she looked like crazy Phoebe from Friends when she ran, I now understood why she had avoided the other trails after seeing them this morning.

I was lost in thought as I ran, not bothering to look up at the person heading my way until they were right in front of me and we were about to collide.

"Hey, watch it," a woman shouted, moving to the side before she plowed into me.

I looked around, noticing that I was running down the middle of the trail instead of off to the side, so there was room for her to pass.

She gave me a dirty look, then kept going.

My heart thumped wildly in my chest as I bent over and

tried to catch my breath. I had my hands on my knees, feeling like my lungs were about to explode when I heard footsteps approaching me.

"You alright there?" Maggie asked, coming to a stop beside me.

"Yeah," I panted, standing upright, so I didn't look like a total spaz. Hell, if I could barely handle running in the cold, how would I possibly think that I could handle a woman like Maggie? Her age definitely showed as she bounced in place in front of me, keeping her heart rate up before she took off running again.

"I take it you don't get out here and run much?" she asked, her voice sweet and the perfect pitch to make my dick twitch in my pants. *Traitor.*

"I used to run a lot in New York City," I panted, trying not to show my struggle. I placed my hands on my hips, hoping my broad frame would help me look manlier than I felt.

"Well, Whiskey Mountain is a lot different. I'm sure you're used to running on flat ground back home, not the incline you decided to go up today."

She nodded behind me so I turned and saw what she was talking about. I had been so lost in thought that I hadn't noticed the change in the trail as it climbed the side of the mountain.

"Fuck," I muttered, running a hand down my face. "Honestly, I was a little distracted and hadn't paid attention."

She smiled and tucked a strand of wispy brown hair behind her ear.

"I'm finishing up if you want to run down with me," she offered, eyeing me cautiously as if she was worried that I was going to pass out in front of her. "Unless you're a glutton for punishment and want to keep going up."

"Did you go all the way up?" I asked, pointing to the steep incline behind her.

"Yeah, but I'm used to this trail. It's one of the few that rarely gets covered in ice because the sun constantly melts it."

I nodded, unsure of what to say. Of course she could handle this stupid trail. Her body was sculpted to perfection, and her ass filled out the skintight workout pants that looked like they were painted to her body.

"So, do you wanna do it together?" She raised her brows and waited for my answer.

I felt my head spinning, wondering how she could possibly know that I wanted to fuck her. Was it the thick, hard rod that was threatening to poke out of my gray sweatpants? Or did I have the words *I wanna fuck you* written on my head?

"Are you sure you're okay?" She tilted her head to the side and placed her hands on her hips as her eyes narrowed at me.

"Oh, yeah," I sighed and tried to shake it off. "Sorry. What did you ask?"

If she was really propositioning me on the side of a mountain, I needed to know for sure. If not, I was pretty sure I was about to see a bright yellow light calling me home and that this was just some bizarre hallucination to comfort me before death pulled me in.

"I asked if you wanted to finish your run with me," she said slowly, as if I was stupid. Which, by the way—I was. "Unless you were determined on finishing the run up, then back down. It's up to you."

"The run," I mumbled, spitting words out of my mouth before I could think about them. "You want to run with me, not do me on the side of the mountain."

I shook my head, forcing the stupidity out. When I looked up at her, her blue eyes danced with mischief, and I knew that she had heard everything I'd meant to keep in my head.

"Yeah, we should make our way back down."

"Okay," she said softly. "Whenever you're ready."

My body already felt tired, so the thought of running back down the mountain sounded terrible, but it wasn't like we could just stay up here all day. It was already midday, but soon the sun would start to set, and I couldn't imagine anyone would want to get stranded out here willingly.

"You can go ahead of me," I offered, not wanting her to watch me.

"It's okay, I don't mind bringing up the rear." She winked playfully.

"Is that code for you want to check out my ass?" I joked, walking beside her as she led the way down.

"I mean, I can't say I won't look if that's what you're asking."

"You're such a pervert." I winked, instantly regretting that I was flirting with her again when I saw her reaction to it.

"What can I say? It's the sweatpants. Every guy knows that you don't wear gray sweatpants unless you want women to check you out. Heck, even guys."

I turned to look at her, wondering what the hell she was talking about.

"Am I going to regret asking you what that's supposed to mean?" I asked, picking up my pace as she lightly started to jog. I knew that she was easing into it for me, and while I hated it, I also appreciated it.

"Oh, come on, *everyone* knows about it! It's in all of the romance books, in magazines—it's not a secret!"

"Is this like the whole banana and increased libido thing?"

She studied me for a moment, then shrugged.

"Guess you'll have to look it up and find out for yourself." She gave me a coy smile and then took off running down the mountain, giving me the perfect view of her ass as I involuntarily chased after it.

<u>Eleven</u>
Maggie

The run down the mountain was a lot more enjoyable, and I was thankful to see that Owen seemed to be doing better than he was when I first found him. In the two months since he'd been in Whiskey Mountain, I hadn't seen him running on any of the trails, so it didn't surprise me that he was blindsided by the steep incline on this one.

If you weren't from around here, it was easy to miss because you didn't see how intense it got until you were already halfway up the hill. Personally, I loved it because it pushed me when I really needed it—and today, I definitely needed it.

"You doing okay?" I asked as we slowed at the bottom of the hill and stepped to the side so we were off the trail. I took a long drink of water and focused on him as his breathing evened out.

"Yeah, thanks."

He seemed a little winded still, but I could tell he didn't want to be the center of attention right now, so I looked away and gave him a few minutes.

"Do you do this often?" he asked, nodding to the hill behind us.

"Not all of the time. I tend to stick to the flat trails that run behind the strip mall, but this one is my favorite when I need to clear my head or after I've over-indulged and need to work off some of the calories." I laughed but didn't miss it when his eyes roamed over my body.

He didn't say anything but did move his eyes away from my tits. *So, he's a boob guy. Good thing I have plenty to offer in that department.*

I looked up at the sky, admiring the colors changing as the sun started to set.

"Do you have dinner plans?" I blurted out, startling both of us.

"Dinner plans?"

"Yeah, you know—like sitting down and having dinner with someone? Or going somewhere to eat?"

"No…." There was an uneasiness in his voice that matched the tension tightening his shoulders.

"Well, how about we go grab a bite to eat?" I suggested, trying to keep my voice as neutral as possible so I didn't scare him off. He was sending mixed signals left and right, and I had no idea what to think. First, he ogled my body like it was the first time he'd ever seen boobs, and now he was acting like I had offended his people by asking to share a meal. "I'll pay," I added, trying to keep my smile from getting too big.

"Thanks, but…." He scrubbed a hand down the thin hair that dotted his jaw. "I don't think it's a good idea."

"Relax," I laughed. "It's not a date; you don't have to be so nervous."

He eyed me suspiciously.

"I just thought because we were both done with our run, and neither of us have eaten dinner, that maybe we could go somewhere together. Sometimes it gets boring eating by yourself." I tried to keep any hints of sadness out of my voice but failed. "Plus, I owe you for all of your help with Leroy the other day."

I rocked back on my heels and held my hands in front of me, holding the water bottle.

He waited me out, the decision warring through his brain while he struggled to decide. Finally, he sighed heavily and let his shoulders fall.

"Did you have somewhere in mind?"

I clapped my hands excitedly and let out a slight squeal.

"Yay! I know the perfect place!"

I couldn't tell if he was as excited about it as I was or if he was simply trying to pacify me, but he followed me nonetheless until we got to the now empty parking lot. I had thought about asking him if he wanted to ride over together, but given how he had reacted to my dinner invite, I didn't want to overdo it.

He followed me to Main Street, and we were both lucky to find parking on the street, which was rare and unusual. I should have known then that this wouldn't turn out how I thought it would.

When we got out and walked up to the door of La Salsa, there was a sign on the front that it was closed to a pipe bursting earlier in the day.

I frowned and stared at it, disappointed that I wasn't going to get my chips and salsa fix tonight after all. I had run my ass off, and that was supposed to be my treat, along with a refreshingly cold margarita.

"Damn it," I muttered, rubbing the back of my neck.

"Is there somewhere else you want to go instead?" Owen asked, though he kept staring at the sign and not at me.

"I don't know. It's getting late, and everything in town will be closed soon." I folded my arms over my chest and tried not to sound too whiney. "I really wanted their tacos."

He arched a brow and finally turned to look at me.

"Tacos?"

"They have THE BEST tacos. They're deliciously mouthwatering, and I earned them, along with a margarita."

He rubbed his lips together and then turned to look at me.

"I can make tacos."

"What?" I felt the grin spread quickly across my face. For sure, I thought he would run the first chance he got, but here he was, offering to cook.

"I know how to make tacos. We can stop by the market before they close and grab the stuff we need. I don't mind cooking."

"Who are you, and what have you done with the *real Owen*?" I teased, bumping my elbow against his.

"This is the *real* Owen," he laughed.

"The real Owen seemed reluctant to have dinner with me tonight, and now he's offering to cook for me. Just seems a bit off, that's all." I smiled up at him as we walked back to our cars.

"Well, for the record, the real Owen loves to cook and rarely does so anymore. Plus, you seemed so disappointed; I couldn't look at that sad puppy look on your face for another second."

My heart fluttered inside my chest, and I had to remind it that this wasn't anything to get excited about. Owen was just being friendly; it didn't mean he was interested in me.

"So, do you want to go to the market with me so you can pick out your margaritas? I don't know if you want super fruity or regular." He shrugged, and I could tell that he was back to feeling nervous.

"Sounds good. I'll follow you over."

He nodded and then got into his truck while I climbed into mine. Tonight was going to be fun; I could almost guarantee it.

Twelve
Owen

Shopping with Maggie was more fun than I would have imagined. Her face lit up as we ventured down the candy aisle, and I watched as she tossed a few bags of chocolate into her cart. I had insisted on buying the stuff to make dinner, but she had quickly objected and informed me that she was paying.

I took the liberty to pick out the meat and fixings while she perused the alcohol section and grabbed stuff to make margaritas. Granted, there were bottles of premade ones, but she made a sour face and told me that only crazy people drank those.

Once we had everything we needed—along with some items that we didn't—we checked out, and I loaded the groceries into her vehicle.

"Did you want to come to my place?" she offered after I stuffed the last bag in the backseat on the floor.

"Sure." I shoved my hands into my pockets and remembered the comments she had made earlier about wearing these damn sweats. Suddenly, her eyes trailed down at the movement and locked onto my crotch.

I knew I should have looked away or moved, but I didn't. For a fraction of a second, I enjoyed standing there, knowing she was just as attracted to me as I was to her. Even though I couldn't act on it, it was reassuring to see that it was mutual.

"Okay," she said, shaking her head and clearing her throat. "You can follow me if you don't remember where my house is."

"I remember."

My voice was thick as my cock hardened. Her thick lashes fluttered as she looked up at me.

"I'll see you there in a few minutes."

Her voice was soft and whispery, making me wonder what she would sound like in the middle of an orgasm. Would she be one of those girls who were shy and quiet, or would she be loud and vocal, screaming my name as I pleasured her?

I quickly adjusted myself once I was in my truck and followed her the short distance to her house. Once there, I helped her carry the groceries in and followed her lead on where to put them.

"Pans are in there," she said and pointed as we walked through the kitchen. "Spices are in the cabinet next to the stove. Help yourself to whatever you need, and I'll be back to help in a few minutes."

She smiled, then rushed down the hall and slipped into the bathroom.

I grabbed the stuff that I needed and got started.

It had been a while since I had anyone to cook for, and I had gotten so busy with work that I rarely took the time to do it for myself.

While the beef cooked in the pan, I took the time to finely chop an onion and tossed some in with the meat while keeping the rest to the side for salsa. I loved fresh ingredients and was surprised by what I was able to find at the market this time of year. In New York, we had access to a lot more than I imagined a small town in rural Montana would have.

While the meat was cooking, I prepared the salsa and then put it in the fridge to keep it cold. Maggie insisted that she was good with just tacos, chips, and salsa; therefore, we didn't grab anything for the sides. I knew that tacos were plenty for me, though I might have been thinking about another type of taco—as well as thinking with my dick—when we were discussing it.

The bathroom door opened, then Maggie padded down the carpeted hallway into the living room. She bent down to check on Leroy before joining me in the kitchen.

"I chopped up some lettuce for the tacos and put some aside for Leroy," I said, pointing to the plate I had made for him while she was cleaning up.

"Thank you, that was very thoughtful of you."

She took the lettuce and placed it in his terrarium, giving him a soft pat on the shell.

"Okay, what can I help with?" she asked, wiping her hands on the shorts she was wearing.

Was she trying to kill me?

I thought she looked amazing in the running gear she had on earlier, but this was even more erection-inducing.

It was the middle of winter and freezing outside, though her house was a little warmer than normal, so I could understand her wearing the flimsy shorts. I tried to convince myself that she was only wearing them because it was toasty in here and not because she was trying to seduce me.

"Owen?"

I turned my head and found her watching me with a slight smirk on her face.

"Yeah?"

"I asked what I could help with." She grinned, and I knew that she knew what she was doing to me.

You could sit on my face and let me eat the taco that I really want.

"Umm," I stuttered, turning my focus to the stove as I stirred the meat that was just about done. "I think I've got it all covered. Dinner should be ready in a few minutes."

"Okay. I'll make us some margaritas then."

She moved around me, making the air smell like coconuts.

I turned the burner for the meat down to warm and grabbed another pan to fry the tortillas. My goal was to stay in my area and not venture into hers, but when I turned to get the oil from the cabinet, my chest collided with her head.

My hands reached out to brace her, feeling the curves of her body against mine.

"Sorry," she laughed. "I was trying to get the glasses out of the cabinet."

"Here, let me."

I knew that in order to do it, I had to let her go, yet my fingers dug deeper into her skin. I could swear that I heard a soft moan escape her lips when I did.

She was fire, and I was about to get burned.

I cleared my throat and stepped to the side as I avoided looking at her.

"Which ones?" I asked once I had the cabinet opened.

"The short ones with the blue rims. They're my favorite."

Blue was my favorite too—like the color of her eyes. Though I didn't love the blue balls I was getting from being around her.

I grabbed the glasses and set them down on the counter, too afraid that I might accidentally drop them if our hands brushed against each other.

"There you go," I grumbled, then quickly turned the other way and checked on the meat that didn't need to be checked on.

Maggie made her way over to the fridge and began filling a pitcher with ice. Once she was on the other side of the kitchen, I grabbed the oil and started frying the tortillas.

Everything smelled delicious, and my stomach growled in anticipation. I stacked the tortillas on a paper towel to soak up the excess grease and then grabbed the fixings and salsa from the fridge. Everything was set out and ready to go by the time she finished mixing the margaritas.

She smiled and took another sip before walking over and handing me a small cup with liquid in it.

"Try it and let me know if it needs more tequila?" she asked, lifting it toward me.

I took a small sip, but it wasn't enough to determine whether or not it needed more alcohol. Instead, I lied and said that it was fine. I didn't know how much she had put in the pitcher already, but I didn't want either of us to get drunk tonight. Hell, I wasn't even planning on having a drink, but it felt like it would be rude to decline now that she'd already prepared a glass for me with salt on the rim and a lime wedge.

"Dinner's ready," I said, handing the cup back to her.

"Perfect timing," she replied happily as she set the empty cup in the sink. "We can sit on the couch since I don't have an actual table to eat at."

"Sounds good."

We fixed our plates and then sat down. Maggie pulled the coffee table closer to us, then lifted the top that extended into a table for us to eat on.

"Very nice." I nodded and scooted closer to make sure I didn't drop any food on the rug beneath us.

"Thanks. I don't have people over often, so I've never needed a lot of furniture. Then I got Leroy, and he took up any extra space I had," she laughed. "But this works for me, and the couch is my favorite place to sit anyway, so I can't complain."

"I don't have a lot of furniture either. Just what came with the house when I rented it. I haven't had a need to buy anything else."

"Is it weird?" she asked around a bite of taco. "This is amazing, by the way."

She closed her eyes and chewed, moaning not so subtly anymore.

"Is what weird?" I leaned forward and dipped a chip in salsa.

"Being away from your home for so long? Living in someone else's house and trying to make it yours. Does it get lonely?"

She wiped her mouth with a napkin and watched me as I thought about it.

"Honestly, it doesn't feel much different other than being surrounded by other people's stuff instead of my own. I miss my bed, but as far as being lonely, it's no different than it was when I was in the city."

Her head tilted to the side, and a frown fell on her face. She set her taco down and turned toward me, facing me head-on.

"That's so sad."

I shrugged and took a bite of my taco so I didn't have to say anything. It was sad, but she didn't need to know just how pathetic my life had been after Brittany and I broke up.

"Do you have a girlfriend back home?"

I shook my head and took another bite. I didn't want to have this conversation with her. Not right now. Not ever.

She continued to study me for a few seconds before she turned back to her food and took another bite. We ate in silence for a few minutes, leaving me thankful that she didn't keep pressing for information on why I was such a lonely loser.

Thirteen
Maggie

I was three margaritas in and had quickly learned that Owen didn't want to talk about anything involving his personal life. It felt like playing a game of twenty questions with him, yet almost everything was answered with quick, one-word responses that gave no insight into who he was.

"Do you want a refill?" I asked, nodding to his empty margarita glass clutched in his hand.

He shook his head.

"I'd better not, thanks."

"Okay." I got up, grabbed the pitcher from the counter, and set it down on the coffee table after refilling mine.

I had barely put any tequila in them when I made them, so it wasn't like we were going to get drunk anytime soon. On top of that, we were drinking out of my favorite tumblers, which were half the size of what we would have gotten at La Salsa.

"So, how long do you think you'll stay in Whiskey Mountain?" I asked, pulling the bottom of my shorts down so I didn't expose my ass as I shifted on the couch. I had my knee pulled up to my chest as I leaned into the cushion.

I had taken a quick shower when we got back and then realized I didn't have any clean clothes because, like a dummy, I'd forgotten to move the load I had washed earlier from the washer to the dryer. Granted, I had some clean clothes, but not much I felt comfortable wearing around Owen. I didn't want to look like a granny with my ratty t-shirts that I used to sleep in, which left me looking a bit slutty in booty pajama shorts in the dead of winter.

Granted, it was warm enough in the house to justify it since I'd started keeping the temperature higher in here for Leroy.

"I'm not sure. I'm still waiting for the planning committee and city council to vote on the proposed projects before we can get started, then I'll stick around to see them through. I'd say six months at a minimum, though I expect it to be closer to a year."

I felt somewhat relieved that he would be here for a little while, though I knew I didn't have a reason to be. It wasn't like he was going to start something up with me, nor did I want a casual fling. *Not that I wouldn't want him to fling me over his shoulder and slap my ass with that big, strong, manly hand that I had been admiring all night.*

"So, no girlfriend back home. Do you have a secret wife? Kids?" I wiggled my eyebrows playfully but noticed the way he tensed up at the word *wife*.

"Nope. Nothing."

"Is it something that you want?"

The question flew out of my mouth before I could stop it. I set my glass down and realized that maybe there was more tequila in the margaritas than I had thought. Suddenly, I felt less inhibited with Owen, and while that was thrilling for me, it felt like he was closing himself off even more.

"I used to think that was what I wanted, but things change. I'm not a committed relationship kind of guy. I'm not destined for great love."

He took a sip of his drink and looked away, but the words he'd just said hung in the air around me. Where had I heard that before?

Before I could think about it too much, his phone dinged on the coffee table. He picked it up and frowned before his fingers moved across the screen as he responded to the message.

I took another drink, allowing him the time to deal with whatever had his attention. Suddenly he lowered his phone to his lap and closed his eyes.

"I'm sorry, I need to go deal with something. Thank you for having me over."

He stood up and took his cup to the sink, rinsing it out before putting it in the dishwasher that he had insisted on helping me load earlier.

I followed him to the front door and stood back while he put on his coat and fished his keys out of the pocket. While I had had three margaritas, he had barely gotten halfway through his first one, so I didn't have to worry whether he was okay to drive.

"Thanks again," he said, leaning in for a hug.

I wasn't prepared or expecting it, which left my head tilted back at an awkward angle, allowing his mouth to brush against my throat. My heart beat wildly in my chest as his hot breath skimmed over the skin, leaving fire in its wake. I waited for him to realize and pull away, but instead, he pulled me closer and moved his lips against me, pressing firm kisses and making my clit tingle.

Instinctively, my hands moved up into his hair, holding his head in place while his tongue licked a trail from my jawline down to my collarbone.

He reached down and grabbed my ass, lifting me to his hips before pressing me against the door. I could feel the throbbing hard erection through his sweats and worked myself against it.

"Fuck," he groaned, kissing the other side of my neck and squeezing my ass harder.

I could feel the heat and wetness pooling between my legs. I hadn't been with a man before, but I'd also never felt this turned on by one before, either.

While I used to tell myself that I'd held out this long on having sex because I wanted to find someone who I was in love with to share my first time with, part of me now wondered if maybe I was just holding out for someone that I had insane chemistry with.

Owen had barely touched me, and I felt like I was on the verge of an orgasm. All he would have to do was—

Fuck… That. Right there. All he had to do was slide his fingers under my panties and rub my clit the way he was doing right now.

I dug my nails into his shoulders and bit down on my lip as I tried to keep from coming. He had barely touched me, and I was about to lose it.

There was no way he was this goo—

"Oh my God," I moaned against his neck as his fingers coaxed every last bit of orgasm out of me. My legs trembled as I panted heavily, thankful that he was still holding me up since I didn't trust my legs to do their job now.

"We shouldn't be doing this," he moaned in my ear before nipping it. "I'm too old for you."

"You're not."

"I am. You're still just a baby."

I could feel his dick pressing against my sensitive clit and wanted to give him as much pleasure as he'd just given me. Despite how nervous I felt about the actual sex part, I'd given plenty of hand jobs and blow jobs to know how to get a man off quickly.

"I'm twenty-two and know what I want." I reached down

and grabbed his cock, moaning again at the heaviness in my hand. He wasn't just big—he was the biggest I had ever felt, and I wasn't sure if that was a good thing or a bad thing for someone's first time. Guess we were about to find out.

I pulled the front of his sweats down, along with his briefs, and felt the drop of precum on the tip of his dick as it popped free.

I stroked him slowly, trying to wrap my hand around his girth. He was huge. Massive. I wanted to drop to my knees and take him in my mouth, but I needed him to put me down first.

As I continued to work him in my hand, he planted kisses along my neck, dipping lower toward my chest. God, I wanted this so badly. With one hand, I reached up and tugged my shirt down, exposing one breast.

Picking up on what I wanted, he slid a finger inside the cup of my bra and pulled it down. Then he lowered his head and licked the hardened nipple before sliding it into his mouth and sucking.

I bucked against the wall, moaning as he sucked harder. This was heaven and hell at the same time as my body reacted to his every touch and geared up for another orgasm.

There was no doubt about it, I wanted Owen to fuck me, and I wanted it to happen now.

"Let's go to my room," I panted. "I want you to fuck me."

"We should stop," he mumbled as he worked the other side of my bra down and tortured my other nipple.

"No. I don't want to stop. I want you to fuck me. Now. Be my first."

My eyes were shut as I enjoyed every second of arousing pleasure until it suddenly stopped, and I realized what I had said.

I opened them slowly and found Owen's face hardened as he looked at me. He lowered me to the floor and stepped away, quickly tucking his cock back into his pants.

I pulled my bra and shirt back up, then covered my chest with my arms while I chewed on my lip.

"I, um…." I started but stopped when he held up his hand.

He let his head fall back and closed his eyes.

"First?" he asked, still not looking at me.

My heart was racing again, but this time for a different reason.

"It's not a big deal," I said quietly.

It felt like years before he turned and looked at me.

"I have to go."

I didn't have a chance to say anything before the door opened and slammed shut as he left.

Fourteen
Maggie

I stared at the front door for what felt like an eternity before picking my jaw up off the floor and turning the lock. It wasn't like I had expected Owen to come rushing back in and change his mind, but somehow locking the door made me feel more protected from the hurt he'd just inflicted.

My mind was going a mile a minute, trying to process what had just happened. My body was still humming from the incredible orgasm he'd given me with his fingers, but I hated that it still wanted more.

What do you even know? It's not like you know what it feels like or what you're missing out on by not having sex.

I forced the bitter thoughts away and checked in on Leroy before grabbing my phone that was ringing on the coffee table. I was hopeful that it was Owen calling but found Ramona's name on the caller ID instead.

Deciding that I needed company, I lifted Leroy out of his terrarium and then pressed the button to answer the call.

"Hey," I muttered, plopping down on the couch. Leroy trotted around in front of me, following the path of the light pink flowers on the rug that looked vaguely like berries. I knew he wasn't hungry, given he'd already devoured the food I had given him when Owen was here, but it was still cute to watch him try to eat the rug.

"What's wrong? You sound like someone peed in your Cheerios."

"Nothing," I lied. "What's up."

"Nope. You first. What happened?"

"It's nothing, really."

"You're such a terrible liar. And lucky for you, I have all night."

"Where's Daniel?"

"Out."

"Are you guys fighting again?"

"When aren't we?"

I leaned against the couch and pressed the phone closer to my ear, ready to be a good friend and lend her an ear. They'd had more fights lately, and she'd recently confided that they'd talked about separating. Ramona and Daniel met in high school and had been together ever since, but they both seemed to realize that maybe they'd drifted in different directions.

"I'm sorry. What was it about this time?"

"I asked him about taking a vacation this year, and we argued about where to go. I want to go hiking and explore some of the national parks before I'm too old and don't have the energy to do it. He wants to drink beer and live by the pool where hot girls flaunt around in bikinis."

"Men suck," I muttered, curling my feet underneath me as I pulled my knees to my chest.

"Yes they do. Now tell me what happened. Was it Samuel or Owen?"

"I haven't heard from Samuel since I told him it was over. He hasn't bothered to contact me, and I couldn't be happier."

"Okay," she sighed. "What happened with Owen?"

"I might've accidentally mentioned the *v-word* while we were…. You know."

She gasped on the other end, and I cringed.

"Vin Diesel?"

The laughter erupted out of me before I could stop it.

"No, you dork."

She laughed on the other end, automatically making me feel less stressed about it.

"So, did you guys…."

"No. We didn't get that far. Things were going well, and then I asked him to be my first while I was in the throes of passion."

"Wow."

I scrubbed a hand down my face and felt my face flush with embarrassment again.

"I'm so embarrassed."

"Why? You shouldn't be. If he was doing something that great to get you to come out and ask him to take your virginity, I don't think there was anything to be ashamed of."

I thought about how easily I'd been turned on and how he knew exactly where to touch me to get me off in record-breaking time.

"So, what happened," she asked gently.

"He freaked out and confirmed that I had said *first*. Then he stormed out, and I haven't heard anything from him since."

"Just give him time. Guys freak out easily, and you did say that he's older than you. It's probably been a while since he's talked to someone as *innocent* as you."

"I don't know. I think I'm chasing after something that isn't even a possibility," I admitted bitterly. "Every time I try to get to know him, he's always so guarded. Earlier, when I asked him to go to dinner, he looked like I'd ask him to go on a killing spree with me. I had to rush to reassure him that it *wasn't* a date and that I just wanted to say thanks for his help setting up Leroy's home the other day."

"Maybe he's just naturally shy with people?" she offered. "I mean, he's no Vin Diesel."

"What's your obsession with him anyway?" I laughed.

"He's sooo hot. Just saying, I would do a bunch of illegal shit and race cars just to hang out with him."

"You know that's just for the movies, right? It's not like he does that stuff in real life."

"Don't go ruining my fantasy," she scolded.

"Hey, at least one of us still has them."

I could hear rustling around and then heard Pablo yelling at the cat. *Pussy face. Here pussy pussy pussy.*

"Please tell me that Daniel didn't teach Pablo that," I giggled, imagining how she would explain that to her mother the next time she came to visit.

"Of course he did." She sighed heavily. "So, are you going to reach out to Owen and talk about what happened? I mean, it seems like there's a chemistry there that you both started to act on."

I shifted on the couch and kicked my legs out in front of me.

"I don't know. I honestly don't even know what I would say. It's not like I know him that well, and now I've dropped the V-word and scared him off."

"Maybe he just needs time. Don't write him off yet."

"When I finally got him to open up a little bit during dinner, I asked if he had a girlfriend, and he said no. I joked about him hiding a wife and kid back home, and he tensed up. Then he mentioned that he wasn't a commitment type of guy and that he wasn't—"

Suddenly I had a flashback to the email I had read earlier and realized that Owen had said the exact same thing as the person who wrote to Spill The Beans had said.

I'm not destined for great love.

"What?" Ramona asked, interrupting my train of thought.

"Hold on," I rushed out as I jumped up and grabbed my laptop.

I logged into my email and looked for the ones from *Stupid In Montana*.

My eyes scanned it quickly, looking for anything that might tell me whether it was Owen or not.

"Maggie, what's going on? You can't just leave me hanging!"

"Sorry," I said, scrolling to the bottom of the last email. "I think Owen emailed me."

"To apologize for being a chicken shit and walking out on you instead of taking your v-card? Or to invite you over for a ride on the hard-cock express?"

I pulled my head back and frowned.

"Ramona!" I shrieked, then laughed. "Do you always have to be so crass?"

"Hey, don't blame me. You know you were thinking the same thing. So did he?"

I shook my head, trying to figure out what she was saying, but I was still distracted by the email.

"Did he what?"

"Email you to apologize."

"No." I clicked on the first email and reread it. "I think he emailed the blog anonymously."

"What makes you think that?"

"When he was here, he told me that he wasn't destined for great love. Earlier today, I responded to an email that had come in late last night from someone asking for help but admitting that they didn't really want it."

"Okay…."

"In the email, he writes, *I'm not sure why I'm even writing to you, but I guess that's what a few fingers of whiskey does to some people. I know that I don't need help, but I'm also not sure what to do. I like a woman that I just met, and I find myself feeling drawn to her in a way that I've never experienced with anyone else. The problem is that she's looking for a serious commitment, and I'm not a relationship or commitment type of guy. We're as opposite as opposite can be. No matter how hard I try, I can't get her off my mind. How do I get over someone I was never supposed to allow myself to get attached to in the first place?*"

I paused to take a breath but felt a rush of excitement course through me. This had to be Owen; I just knew it.

"When I responded to his email, I talked to him about giving love a try, and he mentioned that he'd been hurt by his fiancé after she left him on their wedding day and ran off with the best man—who also happened to be his best friend. Then he replied, *this woman, she's light in the darkness. She's the good in a world filled with evil. She's everything I'm not and deserves better than I could ever give her. I'm not destined for great love, and I wouldn't want her to miss out on hers by wasting her time on me.* That's the same thing he told me tonight when I asked him about having a girlfriend."

"Maybe it is him," Ramona agreed. "It definitely sounds like it fits."

"Not only that, but he kept saying that we shouldn't do this when we were kissing. He kept saying how he was too old for me. It was like he was looking for every excuse he could find for why we shouldn't do anything."

"Because he's attracted to you but doesn't want to risk hurting you because he thinks you're looking for a commitment that he can't give you."

"I never told him that I was looking for a commitment."

The line got quiet on the other side then I heard a heavy sigh from Ramona.

"No, but I might have mentioned to him that you were looking for your one true love and that you deserved it after what Samuel did."

I pressed a hand to my forehead, completely forgetting about their conversation in Cool Cats the other day.

"Damn it."

"I'm so sorry," she apologized. "I didn't think about it when I said it. I was so proud of you and your blog that I was gushing about how much you love love and deserve to find it yourself."

"It's okay." I shrugged my shoulders and closed my laptop. "It's not like there was anything there, to begin with."

"I know I've already said it like a million times, but don't rule it out yet. You never know, maybe he just needed a few minutes to process the news."

"Yeah, maybe." I set my computer on the coffee table and watched Leroy head toward my bedroom, probably trying to find more underwear to eat. "I better get going, Leroy is on the loose, and I can't afford to keep buying new clothes."

It was a bullshit excuse to hang up, but I wasn't in the right frame of mind to talk about Owen anymore.

"Okay, I'll check in tomorrow, but if you need anything, you know where to find me."

"Up your ass," Pablo called out. "Up your ass."

The corners of my lips lifted into a brief smile at the rowdy bird, then I hung up and chased after Leroy before he got any ideas from Pablo.

Fifteen
Owen

Monday morning I woke up with a pounding headache from a lack of sleep and an overwhelming amount of regret that weighed a ton sitting on my shoulders. I attempted to stop by the café for my coffee to avoid seeing Maggie, but they were closed due to a family emergency that felt a bit too convenient. It was like the universe was laughing in my face, knowing that I would either give in and go to Spill The Beans or dig my heels in and end up with a migraine.

It wasn't that I didn't want to see Maggie, I did. I wanted to pick up right where we'd left off before she uttered those words that sent me flying through her door.

Did I feel like a total prick for how I handled it? Yes.

Did she deserve better than that? Yes.

But at the end of the day, I was trying to do what I thought was best for everyone involved, including her. She had her whole life in front of her and should have someone who could give her more than I could, especially for her first time.

I'd been sitting at my desk for over an hour, staring at the cup of coffee I'd attempted to make this morning. It tasted like shit. There was nothing special about it, but even the regular black coffee that I got from Spill The Beans tasted better than this. It wasn't that I didn't know how to make coffee—I'd been doing it since I was old enough to make it for my grandpa. But something about this cup tasted more bitter than it should.

I answered a few emails and then jumped on to the Zoom meeting I had with my office in NYC. I was the last one to join, which wasn't a big surprise given that I was moving slower than Leroy on a bad day.

"Alright, now that we're ready to start," Beverly said, pushing her glasses up her nose as she leaned in to read her computer screen. "Let's begin with an update on the Hudson Creek project."

She looked up and stared at the camera as Tim, a guy working out of our Idaho office, began talking about the progress of the development he'd been sent there to oversee. I tried to focus and pay attention, but every time I yawned, I found myself sinking a little lower in my chair.

Next up was an update from Ashley out of our main office. There were some budget details that didn't impact me, so I tuned her out and waited until Beverly moved on to the next person. I was thankful that I didn't have much that I needed to discuss and even more grateful that I was last on the agenda.

"I'm meeting with the mayor and city council tomorrow morning to discuss their decision on breaking ground on the vacant land between Whiskey Mountain and Fallen Oaks. I've also reached out to a referral that I had for local contractors in Fallen Oaks to see if they'd be on board for giving us a quote for the project."

"Sounds great," Beverly said with a smile. "Keep us updated on the final decision, and let me know if you need me to send someone to assist now that it's going to be a larger project than anticipated. I know we discussed you being in Whiskey Mountain for six months, but I imagine this project would extend beyond that. We can discuss options and whether you'd prefer to hand this off to an assistant once it's up and running so you can return to New York."

I smiled, but it didn't meet my eyes. The thought of leaving Whiskey Mountain was something that I had been thinking about nonstop from the moment my flight landed two months ago. Now that I'd been getting to know Maggie more, I felt this uncomfortable feeling in the pit of my stomach at the thought of leaving.

The meeting ended, and I was suddenly starving. It was already afternoon, so I locked my office and went in search of something to eat. I walked a few blocks down Main Street and popped into the deli on the corner. Even though they didn't serve coffee, they had a nice selection of energy drinks in the cooler by the register, so at least I could get some caffeine in me.

I placed my order and stood to the side while waiting for it. The place was busy, but that wasn't unusual. I'd realized that almost every place in Whiskey Mountain felt busy because there weren't that many places to go. But even then, it felt calm and relaxing, unlike the chaotic buzz I was used to in New York City.

No one here bumped into you and kept walking. They didn't look past you as they hurried by.

Instead, it was just like you'd see in those Hallmark movies where people stop to say hi as they pass you or invite you to join them if they see you sitting by yourself to eat. Things that I had never experienced before I came here.

As if proving a point, an elderly couple brushed by me as they headed out the door and stopped to apologize before asking how my day was going. I'd met them a few times at the town hall meetings and knew they were passionate about keeping the current strip mall intact instead of knocking it down.

"Take care; we'll see you at the next meeting," Trixie said with a smile as she allowed her husband to guide her out the door.

"You too; it was nice seeing you."

I smiled and held the door open for them before returning to my spot on the wall.

"Owen," a voice called from over the counter.

I turned to grab my order and almost bumped into another person as they tried to move to the side and out of the way.

"Sorry," I said, stepping back to make room for them.

"Hey," Ramona said, smiling once she noticed me.

"Hey. I almost didn't recognize you without Pablo," I laughed, remembering her from the pet store.

"Yeah, I can't take him many places with me unless I want a slew of curse words tossed around at innocent bystanders."

"That could be fun." I shrugged.

I'd never been a pet person—you know, the whole commitment thing apparently wasn't my thing—but I could see myself with a bird like Pablo. Something about him and his carefree attitude made me almost want to be him.

"A lot of the locals are used to him, but we get plenty of tourists that are not big fans of his potty mouth." She laughed, and I joined her.

"You grabbing something to eat?" she asked, looking over the counter at the guy who was still holding the bag with my to-go order.

"Yeah, just a quick bite. You?"

She nodded, and I noticed a change in how she looked at me. It was almost as if she'd gone from happy to see me to pity, though I didn't know why she would do that.

"Do you want to eat together?" she offered, lifting her brows hopefully.

I reached over and took my order so the guy could get back to work. While I wanted nothing more than to go back to my office and eat alone, something made me reconsider.

From what I could tell, Ramona knew Maggie pretty well, which meant that I might be able to check in to see how she was doing without having to tell her what I did. Though, if they were super close, then Ramona likely already knew what happened, which might be why she had given me that look.

She tilted her head and waited for my answer.

"Um, sure." I pressed my lips into a thin line, suddenly uncomfortable and unsure what to do.

She smiled as if sensing my discomfort and looked around the room.

"There's a table in the back. If you want to grab it, I'll meet you in a few minutes once my order is ready."

I nodded and then took off to grab the table. Once I was situated, I opened my energy drink and took a long sip, hoping the caffeine would give me some sort of magical powers to handle the conversation that I suddenly wanted to have with Ramona but knew that I shouldn't.

By the time she got her order and sat down, I'd already finished my drink and ran off to grab another.

I could tell she was trying to give me space before we started talking, and I appreciated that. We ate in silence, nearly finishing our sandwiches before I got the nerve to speak.

"I fucked up," I blurted out randomly, startling her as she held her spicy tuna wrap to her lips.

She lowered it to the plate on the table and then wiped her hands on the napkin.

"Like with your order? You didn't like the club sandwich?"

I shook my head, feeling stupid.

"Sometimes they don't get the bacon right, so it's not always my go-to. They have a delicious Cubano if you want to try that instead. Or this one is really good if you want to try a bite and see if you like it?" She lifted her food and extended it to me.

"No," I sighed, leaning back in the metal chair and tossing my napkin onto the table in front of me. "I fucked up with Maggie."

She was still holding her wrap in front of her when the realization hit. The way her hazel eyes narrowed slightly told me that she already knew what had happened between us.

"I don't know that she would want me talking about this with you," she said quietly before taking a bite and keeping her eyes on the table.

"I know," I admitted and ran a hand through my hair. "I feel like a complete idiot and don't know what to do."

She continued chewing, wiped her mouth, then spoke.

"Have you thought about reaching out to her?"

I shook my head.

"I've been trying to avoid her from the moment I first saw her." I grinned but not because it was funny. She'd been addicting the second I laid eyes on her, and I should have known from the start that she would be my undoing.

"I hate to tell you, but it's pretty hard to avoid anyone in Whiskey Mountain." I could tell that she was joking, but it was true.

"I know. I just feel terrible about what happened."

Ramona finished her wrap and then took a long drink of water as she watched me.

"Is it because of what happened or because of how you handled it?"

I cringed as I thought about my answer.

"Both."

That was a lie, but it was one that I needed to convince myself to believe. If I allowed my brain to think about how good she felt wrapped around my fingers as she climaxed, I would never walk away, and she would end up getting hurt in the process.

"Then talk to her and tell her that." Ramona pulled in a deep breath, then let her shoulders fall. "Look, I don't want to get in the middle of whatever this is between the two of you, but I feel like I have a small amount of responsibility here too. I should have never told you that Maggie was looking for her one true love. I get that it makes it sound like she's one of those clingy women who are so desperate for love that they jump into relationships without bothering to look first. That's not Maggie. She broke up with her last boyfriend because he was a douchebag who didn't deserve her." She locked eyes with me before continuing.

"He knew she was a virgin and constantly tried to make her feel guilty for not having sex with him. Trust me when I say that Maggie is not someone who does something unless she wants to. So, if she was close to having sex with you and asked you to be her first—it wasn't something that her last boyfriend ever earned, and they'd been together over six months. He wasn't the only guy she'd dated in the past year. Don't get me wrong, it's not like she's going out with guys left and right, but she does get her fair share of guys who are interested in her.

"The thing about Maggie is that she respects herself enough to know what she wants and what she doesn't. That's why she's so good with the advice she gives others. She doesn't encourage them to settle to be happy. She truly believes that you should create your own happiness and not rely on someone else to provide it for you. She's never needed a man for anything in her life. She runs a successful business and enjoys having her blog. *When* Maggie finds her one true love, she won't have to question it because it will be one of those experiences that make heaven and earth move. She deserves to have that, and I'm proud of her for waiting for it. God knows I should have."

She crumpled up her trash and collected mine before she stood up.

"I can't give you advice on what you should or shouldn't do, but what I can tell you is that if you're afraid to get to know her because you're afraid that she's going to fall in love with you, there are worse things that could happen. Being loved isn't a bad thing, and you should want that for yourself too, Owen. We all deserve it; some of us just have to fight harder for it than others. Do yourself a favor and have an honest conversation with her."

She offered a sympathetic smile before tossing our trash and heading out the door. I sat there for a few minutes, allowing the words to circle around in my head with no idea what to do with them.

<u>Sixteen</u>
Maggie

I'd been thankful for a busy Monday to keep me distracted from thinking about Owen, but after the final customer left, I found myself alone in the café with those stupid thoughts that hadn't shut up since he left last night.

Talking to Ramona had been somewhat helpful, though I didn't feel like I had any resolution after we hung up. I knew that she meant well and wanted things between Owen and me to have a chance, but I couldn't shake the thought that maybe this was the universe's way of stepping in and stopping things before I could get hurt.

Maybe I'd finally had enough of my fair share of shitty relationships that I was finally being spared.

I wiped down the counters and restocked the supplies for tomorrow morning before sitting down and turning on my computer. For once, I wasn't in the mood to answer emails about finding love or staying in it. I was bitter and sour from last night, which made it hard to focus on other people's problems.

As I waited for the new emails to finish populating, I heard the text message notification on my phone and picked it up.

Samuel: Hey beautiful, can I take you to dinner tonight?

My stomach curdled at the thought, and my fingers flew rapidly across my phone as I typed out my response.

Me: This number has been disconnected and is no longer in service.

A cheeky grin spread across my face as I slid my phone to the side and opened the first email. It wasn't too heavy, so I went ahead and replied to it, giving them the best advice I could.

An hour later, I'd worked through almost all of the emails when a new one popped up.

My heart hammered in my chest as I read the sender's name and found that it had been sent to the blog, not my personal email address.

Ask Mags,

It seems like I've found myself in a position where I need help again. This time I acted on my instincts and ended up hurting the woman I was trying to stay away from. It seems I can't avoid hurting her, no matter how hard I try.

I've made a fool of myself, and worse, I worry that I've caused her to feel unworthy of the attention and love she so clearly deserves. How do you go back in time and fix something that should have never happened?

--Stupid In Montana

I swallowed hard as the tears slid down my face. If I had any doubt before that this was Owen, this now confirmed it for me.

I knew that he freaked out last night when I asked him to be my first, but I didn't stop to think that he might actually regret it. That hit harder than I could've imagined.

Was it a mistake? If it was, then why did it feel so good?

I chewed my nail as I continued to stare at the email, debating whether to reply or not.

Last night was a night of heavy thinking, and even though

I had enjoyed what happened between us, I found myself going back and forth on whether it was the right thing. Maybe Owen was right that we should have stopped and not let it happen to begin with.

I'd even gone as far as making a list of pros and cons of being with someone like Owen and frowned when I'd seen that there were more cons written on the paper than pros.

Pros:

Attractive

Good with his hands

Makes me feel good

Cons:

Lives in NY

No commitment

Doesn't open up

Older

Afraid to settle down

Has been hurt and has emotional scars

Doesn't want a committed relationship

Doesn't believe in true love

Refuses to commit

Okay, so maybe the commitment thing was a bit overkill, but I couldn't push it out of my head if I'd tried. And trust me, I've tried. The thought of not being with someone that made me feel so electrically charged when they'd touched me like Owen did made it hard to ignore. But I wasn't willing to allow myself to start something based purely on physical attraction, only to have my heart broken by it later.

I inhaled slowly as I steadied myself, then exhaled and began writing my response to his email.

Dear Stupid In Montana,

I'm sorry to hear that. It's hard to put yourself out there and then later feel like you regret what you did.

While you can't go back and fix something that's already happened, you can grow from the experience, which I think you have. You've acknowledged that your actions have had an impact on someone else, and you're more concerned with their happiness than your own. I know a lot of people who still aren't able to do that.

As far as worrying about making her feel unworthy unless you blatantly told her that she wasn't worthy, I wouldn't be too concerned about it. If she's smart, she'll know her worth without having to rely on anyone else to confirm it. Believe it or not, there are people who are able to hold their own in a relationship and don't need anyone else to be responsible for them. That's the beautiful thing about most relationships—you share things together. It's not a job or a duty. You don't have to constantly prioritize the other person's happiness over your own.

If you do decide to embark on a new relationship, you owe it to yourself to find out what makes you happy first. Don't ever rely on someone else to create your own happiness, and don't allow anyone to make you feel responsible for theirs.

I pressed send and swallowed back the tears that threatened to burst free. Whether Owen knew I knew it was him emailing me or not didn't make a difference in how I responded. If anything, I hoped he knew so that it would save us from having an uncomfortable conversation the next time we saw each other. I imagined that wouldn't be anytime soon, given that he'd avoided me all day, and I had gotten a text message from a girl I went to school with, asking if Ramona was cheating on Daniel because she saw her having lunch with the hot new guy in town.

I knew Ramona would tell me about their lunch date when she was ready, but it still irritated me that I had to hear it through the grapevine of small-town gossip first.

I closed my email and shut my computer down before packing up for the day. While I usually enjoyed hanging out and people-watching until it got dark, I wasn't in the mood today. If anything, I was more eager to get home and spend some quality time with Leroy than risk running into Owen when he left for the day.

Seventeen
Owen

I had dated plenty of women to know that Maggie was pissed when I read her email response. I hadn't put my name in the emails when I'd sent them, and thanks to sending them through the blog, it allowed me to post under an anonymous profile. But somehow, deep inside, I felt like she knew it was me.

Hell, it would be hard for her *not* to know that it was me. It wasn't like I had tried to be secretive when I'd sent the recent email, and it basically spelled out what had happened. But I was desperate and wanted to clear the air between us, yet I was too scared to go see her in person.

I knew that I owed it to her to have the conversation face to face, but I didn't trust myself not to try to touch her again. It was like she was an addiction, and I didn't want to succumb.

After talking to Ramona, I knew that she was right about Maggie. She didn't have to tell me how strong and independent she was; I could see it every time I talked to her. From her taking control of getting Leroy set up in his new terrarium to how she navigated leading me back down the trail after I'd gotten myself winded, she never once asked for help. She didn't need to, just like she didn't need me.

When I'd realized I had been wrong about her all along, I'd started to see Maggie differently. She wasn't this young, love-sick, hormonal teenager that was going to turn clingy and require me to do everything for her. She was funny, mature, and successful and genuinely enjoyed my company.

I had been a dick to her by putting her in a box that she never belonged in, to begin with. When I heard that she *loved* love, it instantly put every wall up that I could. Love was the last thing I needed, and a relationship was even further off the table, given that I wasn't staying in Whiskey Mountain.

But something about Maggie changed the way I'd started thinking, and I hated that I suddenly felt so open to the idea of so many things.

Even though I was still much too old for her, it didn't feel like it when we were together. Honestly, she was a lot more mature than most girls her age. Or maybe I just remembered twenty-two-year-olds differently from when I was that age and was obsessed with bedding as many of them as possible.

Maggie didn't act childish, nor did she act her age. If anything, it felt like she was closer to my age. When we talked on our way back from Cool Cats, it was effortless conversation and flowed so easily. Just like it did last night during dinner—after I finally loosened up enough to talk to her.

I had been such an idiot and hadn't realized what I was doing until it was too late. Maggie wasn't someone that I needed to avoid—I was someone she probably should have avoided. I had no idea what I was doing and was so afraid of love that I was willing to push away the first person to take a genuine interest in me. I couldn't remember the last time anyone had asked me questions that they actually wanted an answer to, nor could I remember the last time anyone took the time to talk to me about things that weren't superficial, like the weather.

Ramona was right, Maggie was something special, and I was the dumbass who didn't see it until it was too late.

I grabbed a beer out of the fridge, sat on the couch, and turned on my laptop.

Ask Mags,

It's refreshing to hear your take on relationships, and I admit, I've never given much thought to what would make me happy.

You see, from a young age, I've always been responsible for other people's happiness. My mother was a drug addict, and I was the only one who didn't walk away from her when she tried to get clean. Her happiness fell on me, and if I messed up, she would relapse. There was never anyone else around to show me another way. The only male role model I've had in my life was my grandfather, who was my best friend until he died from a stroke. He taught me to love and take care of my mother, even during the times when I felt she didn't deserve it.

Growing up with a mother who constantly needed me to take care of her, I found myself dating women who needed the same. I was always responsible for everyone else's happiness, which started to feel like a burden, and I resented them for it. I was drowning in the weight of everything that I tried to carry by myself with no one to help.

I was elated when I'd finally found someone who didn't need me to take care of them. I knew then that I'd found my one true love. It was such a rush to know that I could love them freely without having to worry about creating their happiness or sacrificing my own. I was thirty-two, and finally over all of the drama of dating in my twenties.

But then things changed, and I realized it wasn't as easy as I'd thought. You see, she wasn't happy, and it was my fault. I had dropped the ball and didn't stop to take care of her like I had everyone else. I expected too much from her, and in the end, she left me for someone that made her happier than I could.

This is all that I've ever known when it comes to relationships of any kind. They're one-sided, and I'm always the one who is responsible for making sure things work. It's a heavy weight to carry and has left me guarded against starting any new relationships because I'm still exhausted from the ones I've had.

But when you mentioned that relationships shouldn't be a job or a duty and that both people should share in taking care of it, that meant something to me and made me realize that I've been stuck in toxic relationships my entire life and have never known what a healthy one looks like until now.

Granted, I'm not in a relationship with this woman, but that doesn't mean I don't see the possibility now that I've stepped back and examined things.

I believe she can be happy on her own, but part of me wonders if she could be happier with me. I don't know if I know how to love the way she needs me to, but for once, I know that I want to try.

I don't want to be a victim to love anymore. I'm so tired of feeling unworthy of it, and now that I've seen the light in this woman, I don't want to let her go.

Do you think there's a chance she'll let me make it up to her? I know that I'm not responsible for her happiness, but I would like to get to know her if she'd let me because that would make me happy.

Stupid In Montana

Eighteen
Maggie

My eyes burned from crying. Between the recent email from Owen, the slew of unwanted text messages from Samuel, and the chewed-up panties that I'd found Leroy eating in the laundry room, I was at the end of my rope.

I knew better than to let him roam too freely in the house and had completely forgotten to close the laundry room door before I took him out of his terrarium. I also knew that he could pull clothes out of the holes in the hamper, hence how he got my favorite pair of panties.

They weren't sexy or anything special, but they were the softest ones I owned and felt like heaven against my body. They were what I called my "comfties," aka comfort panties. And now they were crotchless with tiny little gnawed through holes all over the place.

Ramona had called a few times, but I'd been cranky and sent her to voicemail. She didn't bother to leave a message, which meant she would call back again. Today was the most Mondayest Monday ever, and I couldn't wait for it to be over.

I checked on Leroy as I passed by to grab the laundry from the dryer, making sure he didn't have any underwear stuck in his shell after he'd tried to crawl through one of the smaller holes he'd made. Right as I'd finished pulling the clean clothes out, I heard the doorbell.

I grunted and headed to the couch, not bothering to go to the door. Whoever was there could leave since I wasn't up for company and hadn't invited anyone over. My parents lived out of state and never just dropped in. I didn't have any friends other than Ramona, and she knew better than to just show up when I was in a bad mood. Besides, she was supposed to be working tonight. That left Owen and Samuel—both of which I didn't want to see.

The TV was on, but the sound turned down as a commercial played. I pulled out a pair of leggings, folded them, then set them on the coffee table as I grabbed another pair. The doorbell rang again, so I ignored it. If it was an emergency, they could go to one of the neighbor's houses.

I kept working through the pile of clothes, relieved that whoever it was seemed to have left because the ringing had stopped. Then suddenly, I saw movement outside the window behind the couch and tossed the clothes on my lap to the floor.

Startled, I jumped up and clutched a hand to my chest.

I lived in small-town Montana where the crime rate was pretty much non-existent, so it wasn't like I had any freaking clue what to do with an intruder outside.

I stood there stupidly staring at the back door as the handle rattled.

"Maggie! Open up!"

I tilted my head to the side and listened again.

"Open up, or I'm going to break a window and come in."

Finally recognizing the voice, I rolled my eyes and opened the back door. Rain came pelting in, spraying me in the face with the gush of wind that whipped by.

"What the hell are you doing?" I demanded as Ramona came in, soaking wet and dripping on the rug.

I closed the door and locked it behind her before reaching into the laundry basket and tossing her a towel.

"You haven't been answering your phone, and you wouldn't answer your door," she replied as her teeth chattered.

"I didn't feel like talking."

I kept my hands on my hips, glaring at her.

"You could have been dead." She shivered again, looking like a frozen popsicle in the middle of my living room.

"Here, put this on," I offered and handed her a clean hoodie.

She turned around and pulled hers off, along with her soaked shirt, and slipped it on.

"Thank you."

I plopped down on the couch and nodded for her to sit in the chair across from me. She sat on the edge, trying not to get it wet.

"What are you really doing here?"

"I came to check on you."

"I'm fine," I lied.

"You've been crying."

"So."

"You're not fine."

"Okay," I sighed with a shrug. "Maybe not right now, but I will be. I've been through worse, this too shall pass."

"I saw the recent Spill The Beans post," she said softly. "Have you talked to him?"

"Not outside of the emails you saw. He replied to mine, but I haven't done anything with it yet."

She leaned back in the chair and waited patiently, not forcing me to say anything more.

Finally, she got up and walked into the kitchen. I turned to see her opening one of the drawers and rummaging around.

"What are you doing?" I asked.

"Looking for the takeout menu from that place you like."

"Which one?"

"The one with the chips and salsa." She pulled out a stack of menus and sorted through them. "There it is! Okay, what do you want from La Salsa?"

I sunk back against the cushion.

"I think they're still closed."

"We won't know unless we try. Now, what do you want, and I'll call in an order."

"You don't have to do that."

"Stop it," she hissed. "I'm here for the night, and we're going to eat tacos and talk through this. So again, what do you want?"

"I'll do the taco trio with guacamole, queso, and an order of chips and salsa."

"Got it," she said, then turned and lifted her phone to her ear.

I had waited for her to give me the bad news that they were still closed. It just seemed fitting that I wouldn't get my La Salsa craving satisfied two nights in a row.

I was still wallowing in self-pity when Ramona came back into the living room and sat down.

"It'll be here in twenty minutes."

My eyes widened in surprise while my stomach growled.

"Wow, I thought for sure they'd still be closed."

"It looks like good things are bound to happen." She gave me a cheeky grin, and I knew there was more that she wasn't telling me.

"Mmmhmm."

I eyed her suspiciously but turned my attention to Leroy before I could give her the fifth degree. He was making a hacking noise from his terrarium, and I knew he would soon be throwing up my underwear, just like he always did.

"Is he okay?" Ramona asked, leaning forward to see him.

"Yeah, he ate my comfties. He'll be fine."

She turned from looking at him to me in disbelief.

"No! He ate your comfort panties?!"

I nodded, feeling the tears sting my eyes again.

"I'm sorry, I know how much they meant to you."

"It's okay. They were just underwear."

"They were the best underwear and will be remembered."

I felt the rumble in my chest as I laughed. It felt good, and I hated that I'd spent so much of my time and energy tonight on being sad and depressed. What had I just told Owen? That he needed to be responsible for his own happiness and not rely on anyone else. Why wasn't I doing the same?

Just because I had been embarrassed and felt a little rejected last night didn't mean I couldn't still be happy. It wasn't like Owen, and I were even dating. We'd just barely started talking, and then things got wildly out of hand when he touched me. It wasn't like this was some relationship I'd invested a lot of time and energy into, so why was I letting it take so much out of me? I was better than this, and I sure as hell was stronger than this.

But there was something different about Owen. Something that I desperately wanted to explore, and now it was gone. Maybe I felt so heartbroken about what happened because, for once, I'd felt something with him that I'd never felt with anyone else, and that gave me hope that maybe he was the real thing. Even if it felt like it was hard to get him to let me in, part of me knew that it would be so rewarding once he did.

"So, are you ready to talk yet, or do you want to wait until you have some tacos in you?" Ramona asked as she studied me from across the room.

"There really isn't anything to talk about. I liked him, but he doesn't feel the same way. He's too old for me and didn't want anything to happen to begin with. We got caught up in the moment, and it was a mistake. But we weren't dating, so I don't know why I'm so hung up on it."

"Maybe because you actually cared for him," she offered softly.

"How do you even like someone that you don't know?" I laughed, realizing how stupid I sounded. "I barely got to know him. I think I was just more obsessed with the idea of who he is than who he really is. I still have no idea what's beneath the layers of barriers he has up, and I don't think I ever will."

"You can like someone without having to know everything about them. There's this strange thing called chemistry— you might've heard about it. Anyway, it's where people just connect—they click in a way they've never clicked with anyone else. And when they do, it's indescribable."

"Chemistry is overrated," I joked as I got up to answer the door. It didn't feel like twenty minutes, but my stomach was excited, nonetheless.

I pulled the door open and frowned.

"You're not La Salsa," I answered dumbly.

"Nope," Daniel said, letting the *p* pop. He held a duffle bag in one hand and a fabric tote bag in the other. He looked past me to where Ramona was sitting with her chin tucked to her chest. "I brought the stuff you asked for."

"Thank you." She didn't look up as she answered him.

I felt awkward standing there, unsure of what to do. He extended the items to me, so I took them and tried to force a smile.

"I know this is what you asked for," he said quietly. "But this isn't what I want. My phone is on if you change your mind and want to talk about it."

She remained quiet and looked out the door she had come in through earlier. I offered a crooked smile and shut the door as he turned around and left.

I walked over, set the bags on the floor beside her, and then took a seat on the edge of the wooden coffee table.

"Okay, your turn to talk. What was that about?"

Her lip quivered as she tried to blink away the tears.

"I left Daniel."

Nineteen
Owen

Two days had passed by without me giving in and going to Spill The Beans for my daily caffeine fix. Instead, the corner market and café had gotten used to me, and I could tell that people around town were already starting to gossip. Last I'd overheard, Ramona was leaving her boyfriend of three years for the sexy new silver fox in town, aka me.

After that rumor, I'd spent a few minutes longer than usual studying myself in the mirror this morning for any traces of gray hair. Not that I was opposed to going gray—I just knew for a fact that I didn't have a single gray hair on my body.

I'd waited patiently for Maggie to reply to my email, but her response never came. I knew at that point that she knew it was me and assumed that Ramona had spoken to her as well. It wasn't like I had any place to be upset about what happened—I was the one who had been holding her at an arm's distance to keep her from getting too close. And look where that got me.

I sat numbly through the day's meetings and tried my best to appear lively when I had my last phone call of the day with the planning committee to discuss their decision about the strip mall. After a unanimous vote, the current strip mall would stay intact, and we would move forward with renovating it and turning it into new shopping and dining options.

It was already after two, and I knew Spill The Beans would be closing soon. Maggie usually kept it open until three, but the past few days, she'd closed earlier and skipped out instead of sitting by the window and writing like she'd done since I first moved here. I hadn't noticed how much I'd been watching her without realizing it until things changed. Suddenly, I knew more about her habits and routines, which made her changing them up feel more directed at avoiding me.

Without giving it much thought, I grabbed my keys and phone from the table and rushed out of the office, determined to talk to her. I had no idea what to say but knew that I owed it to her to say something. Anything was better than nothing at this point. While I thought I was getting what I wanted by pushing her away, I realized that *not* talking to her was more agonizing than allowing myself to get to know her. It didn't mean that we had to sleep together or start anything serious, I just wanted to explore the connection that I'd felt with her because it was unlike anything I'd ever felt before. Unlike most guys her age, it wasn't just about sex. While that was great and all, Maggie could ask me to wait a year before we did anything, and I would because there was more to her than that, and I wanted every single part of her.

When I got to Spill The Beans, I was relieved to see that the lights and the open sign were still turned on. My hand gripped the handle to open it but stopped when I spotted Maggie sitting at one of the tables, across from a guy who was looking at her like she was the most incredible thing he'd ever seen. *Not that I could blame him.*

He reached over and held her hands, tilting his head to the side as he said something that made her giggle. I didn't have to be close to see the blush that traveled up her neck and spread across her cheeks from the words he'd said.

I pulled my hand away and stepped back. Ramona had said something along the lines of Maggie having a lot of prospects. I was stupid for not thinking someone might be lined up and ready to swoop in before I could talk to her. Again, she owed me nothing and had every right to speak to whomever she wanted. It wasn't like we were dating, so

I had absolutely no claim to her, even though I suddenly wished I did.

Staring for a few seconds too long, I finally stepped back and walked away with my head hung in defeat. While I wanted to allow myself to slip into a poor me pity party, I knew that wasn't an option. I needed to be stronger than this. Maggie was just a woman who wasn't in my league, no big deal. Nothing to feel like the world was crumbling around me over.

It was better this way. I could walk away from everything and not have to worry about hurting her in the long run when my work here was over, and I returned to the city. Maggie could find someone to fall in love with who was her age and could give her what she needed. That person wasn't me, and this was exactly how things should be. I was stupid for allowing myself to think that there was anything between Maggie and me other than some explosive chemistry when we touched.

Once back in my office, I closed the door and took a deep breath. I needed to get focused and remember why I was here to begin with.

Van Halen played loudly on my laptop speakers as I cranked through the paperwork to get the ball rolling on the strip mall. I was already ahead of where I needed to be, but that didn't stop me. Something had shifted inside of me, and I felt more driven and determined than ever to see this project through to the end, even if that meant that I would be in Whiskey Mountain longer than anticipated and would have to see Maggie flaunting around her new relationship.

While I had no idea if she was in a relationship, I would still have to see her with someone that wasn't me. The thought of knowing that he was touching her the way I wanted to did nothing to soothe the fire that had been burning in me all afternoon. By four, I had nothing left to work on, so I called it a day and changed into running gear. I'd opted for the gray sweats this morning, hoping that I might run into Maggie, but now I didn't care. It didn't matter anyway.

I grabbed my phone, keys, and earbuds from my desk and headed out the door. There was still at least another hour before the sun started to set, and I had energy to burn.

Twenty
Maggie

"I'm so sorry, Dylan," I said sympathetically as I held onto his hands. "I knew you guys were having some trouble, but I didn't think it was that bad. You should have called me sooner."

He shrugged his shoulders and leaned back in the chair, allowing our hands to fall on the table between us.

"I just feel stupid that I didn't see it sooner. I knew she wasn't that busy and felt like she was making excuses not to see me. I really thought I was being a good boyfriend by surprising her in Fallen Oaks. Guess the joke was on me."

"Stop. She's the only one to blame here. You did nothing wrong."

"I shouldn't have started dating her again, to begin with. It's like I never learn my lesson."

"It's hard to move on when we feel a connection to someone." I pulled my lips into a thin line. "You loved her and weren't ready to give up on that yet."

"No, but I should have listened. You and Ramona told me she wasn't good enough for me, and you were right."

"I don't think we said those words, but yes, we do believe that you deserve better."

Dylan had been one of my best friends since he moved here four years ago. Ramona and I took him in and adopted him as our brother. When he first started dating Kim a year ago, we stayed quiet and prayed that she had changed from the girl we knew in high school. After they broke up the first time, we thought he'd surely learned his lesson. But then Kim pulled the same act she'd used on her other boyfriends, and he took her back.

While I didn't initially want to be the one to come out and tell him that I thought she was cheating on him, I now regretted it. I hated to see him hurting the way he was over someone who didn't respect him and was probably already crawling into bed with the next guy.

"I think I'm just destined to be single for a while. Every relationship I've been in has ended with them cheating on me, and that has to mean something."

I reached over and squeezed his hand again, waiting until his eyes caught mine.

"It means that you haven't found the right person yet. These failed relationships are nothing other than a guide to show you what you deserve and to teach you to appreciate the wonderful parts of a real relationship, so you know what it looks like when you see it. You're only twenty-two; you have plenty of time to find that person for you."

"So," he shifted in his seat and looked around. "What's going on with you? Has Samuel come crawling back yet?"

I crossed my leg over my knee under the table and grunted.

"He doesn't get the message. I've asked him to stop texting and calling me well over a hundred times, and he just doesn't get it."

"Oh, he gets it. He's just determined to squeeze his way back into your life."

"Why do you say that?" I furrowed my brow at the smile plastered across his face.

"Because he's an asshole, and you have something he wants."

"I do?" My eyebrow arched high on my forehead.

"Obviously. You know every guy wants to be able to say that they took *it*. He's no exception. He's hoping that you'll take him back and give him a second chance so he can try again."

I pulled my head back in disgust and scoffed.

"That's both stupid and gross."

"Trust me—I know men my age. He'll stop coming around once he knows that someone else got it. Until then, it's like a challenge, and he wants to win. All men do."

I shook my head but knew that he was right.

"No, not *all* men," I muttered quietly and looked out the window.

"Is there someone new that I don't know about?" he asked, leaning forward with interest. He twirled his finger in the air at me. "I sense new gossip that you're holding out on me."

"No," I waved him off. "I was just saying in general."

His eyes narrowed as he called my bullshit.

"Nope. You're lying. Spill it."

My eyes widened as the guilt etched across my face.

"I'm not lying, I don't know what you're talking about," I laughed nervously.

He gave me one quick cursory glance, then picked up his phone and began typing.

"What are you doing?" I asked, leaning forward to look at his screen before he pulled it closer to his chest and out of my sight.

"Getting the 411."

I rolled my eyes and leaned back in my chair. If he was checking the blog for info, he wasn't going to find anything helpful.

He set the phone down and placed his hands in front of him as he stared at me.

"You can tell me now or wait for Ramona to fill me in. Your choice."

I inhaled sharply, feeling slightly betrayed though I should have seen it coming.

"By the way, I don't need your truck anymore," I said randomly, trying to pull his attention to something else. Anything else.

"No? Why not? Did you decide on something else for Leroy?"

"I actually had someone else help me while you were gone."

He clapped a hand over his heart as if he'd been wounded.

"You went to someone else for help?" he gasped, playing the part of dramatic best friend perfectly.

"I didn't go to them; they just happened to be there and offered to take me."

His phone dinged and he picked it up, glancing at me before reading the message.

"Would that happen to be the new older guy in town that totally fucked up?"

He turned his phone to show me the message from Ramona.

Ramona: Owen—the sexy older guy handling the strip mall. Totally fucked up, and now Mags won't get out of her own way to allow something to happen between them.

I chewed my lip and kept quiet. Double betrayal.

"It's nothing. He helped me get the stuff I needed for Leroy, we had dinner once, then he found out that I was a virgin and booked it out of my apartment faster than a bolt of lightning. There's nothing more to it than that."

"Then why does Ramona think that you're getting in your own way?"

"Because she wants something to happen for me so badly that she can't see the truth of what's actually there."

"Which is what?"

"Nothing. Absolutely nothing. Unlike Samuel, Owen isn't interested in trying to take my virginity. He's so far off from being interested in me that he'd rather bolt out of my house than hear that I haven't had sex before. So see, not all guys are like Sam. Some of them don't even want that from me."

I sank down in my chair and pretended to listen as Dylan listed all of the reasons why I was wrong. It didn't matter; I knew deep down what the truth was.

Twenty-One
Owen

It was amazing how easily you could avoid someone in a small town if you really tried. Granted, I was down to a few slices of bread, some leftover pizza, and a questionable block of cheese, so I couldn't avoid going out for much longer. I needed to do some grocery shopping but knew that the chances of running into Maggie on a Saturday were fairly high given that she'd chosen to close the coffee shop today—not that I'd been by to notice.

I knew it was stupid and childish to avoid her, but it'd been a week since I'd run out of her apartment, and the longer we went without talking, the more awkward it felt. How was I supposed to look her in the eye after having my fingers deep inside of her and act like nothing had happened? Yet I had to do exactly that because the few times I've seen her in passing, she's been with the same guy I saw her in the coffee shop with.

Knowing I needed to get over myself, I grabbed my keys and headed to the store. It was busy with people filling the aisles, but nothing like what I was used to in New York City. I browsed casually, trying to convince myself that I was solely checking out the options so I could plan some meals to cook this week and that I wasn't purposely lingering around in the hopes of running into her.

It was like running hot and cold—I wanted to see Maggie, then I wanted to avoid her. At this point, I didn't know which end was up, and I hated that I felt as indecisive as a kid in a candy shop.

While I knew what I wanted, my head was struggling to convince my heart that it wasn't something I could have. Women like Maggie didn't belong with men like me, and it needed to stay that way. I had to remember that it was selfish to entertain ideas of us together because I was the one who would be walking away and breaking her heart in the process.

I wandered aimlessly down the rice and bean aisle, pushing my cart slowly as I scanned the different options.

"Find anything good?"

I looked up to find Mayor Landing beside me, looking at the shelf that held my attention.

"Um," I frowned and looked closer. "No idea."

She laughed and rested her hand on my shopping cart.

"How are you?" she asked, and I couldn't help but notice something different in her voice. It sounded motherly, which hit me in an odd way, given that my mother was never clean or sober enough to bother trying to be mine.

"Good. Just picking up some groceries. How are you?"

"Great, thank you. I'm helping plan my granddaughter's eighth birthday party and had to come for some last-minute supplies."

I smiled at the way her face lit up when she spoke about her family and then tried to push aside my discomfort of not knowing what that felt like.

I glanced in her cart and noticed an abundance of pink as it overflowed with streamers, balloons, and princess fairy wands.

"It's a princess tea party," she offered, looking down and laughing. "My husband has been groaning nonstop about how our house looks like Pepto-Bismol. He'll be glad once the party is over. My daughter and I felt bad about all of the girly stuff taking over his space that we're sending him to play golf on Sunday while we clean up."

"That sounds like a nice gesture; I'm sure he'll appreciate it."

"If there's anything he loves *almost* as much as his family, it's golf."

I laughed softly, having met him a few times, and knew this to be true from the handful of stories he'd told me.

"Well," she said with a sigh. "I need to finish up my errands before the day gets away from me. It was wonderful to see you."

"You too, take care, and I hope your granddaughter has a great party."

"Thank you. You're more than welcome to join us. It's Saturday at two. Just go down Townsend Drive, and you'll find it—it'll be the only house decked out in pink."

I smiled and nodded, not saying anything so I didn't accidentally commit myself. She gave a little wave and then took off down the aisle to finish shopping.

Deciding that I didn't need rice or beans, I pushed my cart down the aisle and around the corner to the next one when I stopped short to avoid hitting someone.

I didn't have to wait for her to whip around and show me her face to know it was Maggie. Her ass in the tight yoga pants was enough confirmation for me.

My mind raced as I tried to decide whether to pull back and go in the opposite direction before she could see me, but it was too late.

Her eyes widened when she saw me, and I could tell she had been avoiding me, just as I had been avoiding her.

"Hey," she whispered softly, her hands gripping the shopping cart handle tighter.

"Hi."

I stood there, frozen in place, as we stared at each other.

The seconds ticked by, sounding loud in my head as the blood rushed past my ears.

"How are you?" I finally rushed out before I could chicken out.

"Good."

I swallowed hard, forcing the rush of emotion back down. She wasn't as talkative as I remembered her being before, which made me even more nervous.

We continued to stand to the side of the aisle as other customers passed by. No one bothered to say anything, but that didn't mean there weren't curious glances and hushed whispers.

"I'm really sorry about what happened," I said quietly, leaning toward her so she could hear me.

"Don't be. It's fine."

My shoulders tightened, knowing that it was anything but fine. She wouldn't be this stiff and guarded toward me if it was. I'd hurt her, just like I wanted to avoid all along.

"Maggie," I sighed and ran my hand through my hair. "It's not fine, and I owe you an explanation."

"No, you don't. You were the one who told me that we should stop; I should have listened."

I pushed my cart to the side and took up the space beside her so I could talk without everyone else listening.

"Yes, I said that. But Maggie, that doesn't mean that I regret what happened. I've been stuck in my head trying to figure this thing out, and I still have no idea what any of it means. I'm completely lost and out of my element here. You're twelve years younger than me, and I don't want to take advantage of you. Not only that, you're—"

"A virgin. I get it," she snapped, looking sharply at me then around to make sure no one else heard her. "I was stupid for letting anything happen as well. It wasn't just you. We both made a mistake. It won't happen again."

She reached for her cart as I stepped forward and blocked her. Trying to respect her space, I put my hand on the shopping cart to keep her from leaving.

"Despite everything telling me that I should leave you alone and walk away, I find that incredibly hard to do," I admitted.

She arched a brow and narrowed her eyes.

"There's no prize to be won, so feel free to move along."

I pulled my head back and frowned. What the hell was she talking about? Prize??

Then suddenly, it clicked.

I leaned forward, forcing her back against the shelf of canned goods behind her. I looked over my shoulder to make sure no one was watching as I gently placed my hand on her hip and whispered in her ear.

"Maggie, rest assured that I am not interested in *winning* anything, nor do I care whether you're a virgin. If you decided to go have sex with someone else, just to keep me from being able to say that I took that from you, be my guest. I'm not interested in this thing with you because I want to take your virginity. I'm interested in you. Who you are. What you like. And more importantly, because of how you make me feel when you're around me. So let me just make this abundantly clear—if given a chance with you, I will NOT initiate sex. That power is yours, Maggie. I respect the fuck out of you for knowing what you want and not giving that part of yourself to just anyone."

I pulled back slowly and allowed my hand to fall to my side. Her breathing had increased, and her pupils were dilated, matching what I imagined mine now looked like as well. I felt intense chemistry every time I touched her, and this was no exception.

"Owen, I can't," she started before I held up a hand and cut her off.

"I know that I hurt you, Maggie, and I'm sorry. I hate myself for causing you any kind of pain. But you can't deny that there's something between us. You feel it too, I can tell by the way you react when I touch you."

She leaned away from the shelf and straightened her back, taking a deep breath and slowly letting it out as she tried to compose herself.

"Yes, there may be something between us *physically*, but that's not enough for me."

My heart dropped.

"While I admit that I would love nothing more than to explore whatever this is between us, I can't allow myself to do that. At the end of the day, I'm still the same girl you were trying to avoid—the one who loves love and wants her happily ever after someday. It's not fair to me when I know it would be temporary."

"I know," I said softly, flexing my fingers to keep from reaching for her again. "But plenty of people have long-distance relationships."

My eyes locked onto hers, begging her to listen.

"I know, but that's not the real problem."

"Okay," I took a shuddered breath. "What's the problem? I know there's a way we can solve it."

She took a step back as if she needed more space from me to get her words out.

"At the end of the day, I'm still someone who is going to want more than what you're willing to give to me. I want someone I can spend forever with and be committed to."

"I'm not afraid of commitment," I said quickly. "I know that I thought I was, but you've made me realize that I felt that way because I didn't have anyone worth committing to."

She shook her head as tears welled in her eyes.

"I know that it was you emailing me. *Stupid In Montana.*"

I let my shoulders fall and looked away.

"I don't blame you for having a hard time committing, given what happened with your fiancé. On top of that, you had a childhood that required you to take care of your mother. You said it yourself that you've never been in a relationship with anyone that wasn't toxic. I get it, and I'm sorry you've had to go through all that."

I rubbed my lips together, feeling the anxiety bubbling to the surface.

"But I can't willingly look away and pretend I don't know any of this. My mother taught me to pay attention if someone shows you who they are. You've said countless times that you're not a commitment type of person and that you don't feel like you're destined for great love."

"I didn't know any better at the time," I whispered, hating where this was going.

"I know. But the moment something happened between us, you freaked out and left. You were scared that my being a virgin meant that I would automatically cling to you and that you would have to take care of me, even though I hadn't asked you to. You were so quick to flee because there was the possibility of commitment. I can't look past that, Owen. It's not fair to me, and honestly, it's not fair to you, either. We both deserve happiness, but I don't believe that it's going to come from each other. We're too different and want different things out of life."

I covered my mouth with my hand, then allowed my fingers to trail down the scruff that dotted my jaw.

"I wish you the best, Owen. I really do."

She smiled sadly and walked away.

Twenty-Two
Maggie
One Week Later

"There, yeah, that's it."

"Are you sure that's the right hole? It feels a little tight."

"It's supposed to be tight."

"This tight??"

"Yes, now push it in harder. All the way."

"Ouch!"

"Okay, I'm almost in."

"You're going to have to go deeper. I can't feel anything."

"That's not what a guy wants to hear."

"Funny," I laughed, wiggling my butt on the floor to scoot to the side as Dylan stood over me and tried to line up the top of the cage that we were helping Ramona build for Cool Cats.

"Okay, push down hard," Ramona directed with the instruction manual in front of her.

"I love how we're doing all of the hard work, and she gets to stand there and bark orders at us," I mumbled.

"Hey, *she* is buying you tacos and margaritas as soon as this damn thing is built."

"Did you really need to go all out and get the biggest setup they had?" Dylan asked, stepping back to look at his work.

It was over the top big and could easily house a hundred parakeets. For now, it was going to be Pablo's new home since Ramona and Daniel had officially split, and she was planning to convert the storage room at Cool Cats into a living space for herself. The building already had a bathroom and full kitchen in what she called the breakroom, even though there were no other employees for her to give a break to.

"I wanted him to have the best cage there was since he was being uprooted again. Poor guy hasn't had any real stability in the past six months, and I know that it stresses him out."

"So, have you decided to adopt him yourself?" I asked, moving the empty boxes out of the way so we could clean up and go get food.

"Yeah, he's grown on me, even with his foul mouth."

"Foul mouth. Foul mouth. Bad bird. Who's a naughty bird."

We all looked over and laughed at Pablo as he bounced around on the outside of his old cage.

After Ramona got him situated and made sure he couldn't escape, we piled into Dylan's car and headed to La Salsa.

I bobbed my head as the music played over the speakers while we waited for our waiter to return with our margaritas. A young kid passed by a few minutes later to drop off glasses of water, along with two baskets of chips and salsa. I wasted no time digging in and shoving one in my face when I looked up and saw Owen walk in.

My hand froze in front of my face, and my jaw dropped as I stared at him.

"What?" Ramona asked, then turned around and noticed him. "Oh."

"Have you guys talked since you ran into him at the supermarket last week?" Dylan asked quietly as all three of us continued to watch him.

I couldn't focus on anything other than how the army green sweater wrapped tightly around his chest as he slid into a booth across from a woman.

He was here on a date. He'd done what I told him to and moved on.

"No," I replied so quietly that they both leaned forward to hear me. "He hasn't been in for coffee, and I haven't seen him around town until now."

"Guess he got the message, loud and clear." Ramona frowned in his direction.

"It's what I wanted." I shrugged as if it didn't matter and popped the chip into my mouth.

Ramona and Dylan continued talking about Owen while I tried to wash my worries away with salsa. No matter how hard I tried, I couldn't quite shake the jealousy I felt whenever my eyes traveled in his direction.

It was stupid to be this upset over something I'd never had. Sure, he'd given me the best orgasm of my life, but that was no reason to obsess over him.

Dinner had carried on uneventfully, and I was thankful that the conversation had shifted from Owen to Ramona and Daniel's split. I hated to see either of my friends hurting, but I was pleasantly surprised by how well she was handling it. She'd laughed, and cried, and then laughed some more. I wasn't sure that she had technically processed everything yet, but it was nothing that her second margarita couldn't help.

"Okay, truth or dare," Dylan said around a mouthful of sopapilla.

"Come on, aren't we too old for this game?" I whined and popped a bite into my mouth.

"No. We're not too old. We're young and free and careless. And between the two of you, you're depressing, and we need to liven the night up. So pick one—truth or dare."

"I'm not playing," I shook my head.

"Fine, dare," Ramona said, jutting her chin out. "I could use a little adventure in my life these days."

Dylan wiped his hands on a napkin and then rubbed them together excitedly.

"Alright, I dare you to go over to the two guys sitting in the corner and ask one of them out."

Ramona lifted in her seat to get a good look at them.

"They're out of towners, I already checked." He gave her a pointed look.

"Fine," she tossed out, then got up and walked over.

I didn't bother to look back and see what she was doing because it just so happened to be that they were sitting at the table next to Owen's. I had a feeling that Dylan chose them on purpose because of where they were seated and wanted no part of it. I was also suspicious that Ramona only agreed to it so she could get closer to Owen and his date, given that she wasn't anywhere near ready to think about dating again already. They'd only been split up for a little over a week, and her wounds were still fresh.

I waited a few more minutes, then pulled my wallet out of my purse and tossed a few bills on the table.

"I hate to be a party pooper, but I'm going to head out," I said quickly. "Tell Ramona I'll call her later."

I darted out of the booth before he could stop me.

Twenty-Three
Owen

I knew it wouldn't take long before people started whispering and gossiping once I stepped foot in La Salsa. I hadn't expected that Maggie and Ramona would be there as well, either. I noticed that the same guy I'd been seeing her with was sitting with them too, but on the other side of the booth and not next to her.

I was halfway through my dinner meeting when I spied Ramona talking to the guys at the table next to me. She'd bent down to ask something, but her hazel eyes locked onto mine instead. I tried to look away but couldn't. There were so many questions I wanted to ask her.

Once she was finished getting one of the guy's phone numbers, she walked around and stopped in front of my table. I straightened my spine and forced a professional smile across my face.

"Fancy seeing you here," Ramona said, glancing between me and the woman across from me. I knew what she thought was going on. It was the same thing that had gotten under Maggie's skin and made her twitchy until she finally got up and fled out of the restaurant.

"You too," I said coolly. "Ramona, this is Bellamy Rhodes. She's starting a bed and breakfast in Fallen Oaks, so we're discussing some business opportunities. Bellamy, this is my friend Ramona. She owns Cool Cats, it's a—"

"You own Cool Cats?!" Bellamy shrieked, extending a hand out to Ramona.

"I do. It used to be a speakeasy that my grandpa owned, so I kept the same vibe and turned it into a pet shop."

"I've been there once, and it's amazing!"

I leaned back in my seat and let the two girls talk for a few minutes, thankful that I didn't have to bother explaining to Ramona who Bellamy was.

I was about to tell Ramona that we needed to get back to business when Bellamy's phone dinged.

"Sorry, I need to get going," she said, setting her phone down and reaching for her purse.

"Dinner is on me," I said, holding my hand up to stop her. "Thank you for meeting with me and sharing your experience. I appreciate it, and I'll be in touch as soon as I can set up a meeting with Mayor Landing."

"Sounds great, thank you. It was nice to meet you, Ramona."

Bellamy got up and left, her spot quickly filled by Ramona.

I was about to say something about needing to leave too, but she held her hand up and stopped me.

"I won't keep you here all night," she said as if reading my mind. "I just wanted to check to see how you're doing."

"I'm fine," I lied. She didn't need to know that I'd been miserable ever since I ran into Maggie at the grocery store. Nor did she need to know that I hadn't gone through half of the stuff I'd bought because I no longer had an appetite, hence the half-eaten plate of food that sat in front of me.

"You know she's just as depressed as you are," she said softly.

"I'm trying to give her what she wants."

"She doesn't know what she wants," a deep voice said behind me.

I looked up to find the guy I'd been seeing with Maggie standing there.

"Mind if I join you guys? It was getting pretty lonely at the table by myself."

"Be my guest." I extended my hand to the other side of the booth where Ramona was sitting.

"I'm Dylan, Maggie and Ramona's best friend," he said as he reached his hand out to me. "I'm the guy with the truck that was supposed to help her with Leroy's terrarium."

I nodded as it clicked into place.

"Well then, I guess you already know everything about me."

He shrugged nonchalantly.

"I know what I need to know."

"And what's that?" I asked, leaning back against the booth.

"That Maggie is head over heels in love with the idea of being in love, yet she won't get out of her own way to give this thing with you a chance. It's like now that she has the possibility of actually finding it, she's running scared in the opposite direction."

I chewed the inside of my cheek and folded my hands in front of me.

"I don't know what to do," I admitted. "She has it set in her head that it won't work between us. I know that it's my fault, I was the one who told her that I wasn't someone who wanted a commitment, and then I freaked out when she told me…."

"What do you want now?" Ramona asked.

"I want Maggie." It felt good to get it off my chest and say it out loud. "I don't know anything other than I can't stop thinking about her. I've never felt this way about anyone before, and it scares me, but the thing that keeps me up the most at night is the thought of not having her at all."

"So tell her that. Make her listen." Ramona smiled as if she had the answer to life's biggest problems.

"It's not that easy," I sighed. "She won't listen to me. She's already convinced herself that it won't work, that I won't be able to commit to her and give her what she needs. I literally have no idea how to prove to her that I can commit and that I'm in this for the long run. Between my past track record with relationships and living in NYC, it's kinda hard to show her that I'm willing to try."

"How long before you have to go back?" Dylan asked.

"Now that the Mayor wants to discuss additional projects, I expect to be here at least twelve months, if not longer."

"That's plenty of time to show someone you can commit to them," Dylan noted.

"But how? She won't give me a chance. Aside from buying a house to show her that I'm here for the long run, I'm out of ideas. And while real estate is a hobby of mine, I don't know that I'm ready for *that big* of a commitment right now."

"No, maybe nothing that drastic, but I have an idea," Ramona squealed with a mischievous grin.

Twenty-Four
Maggie

Ask Mags,

My girlfriend recently broke up with me because she's convinced I'm obsessed with sex. It's not like I'm sitting around watching porn twenty-four hours a day, but it wouldn't hurt for us to have it at least once a day. I have needs, and it feels like she's not bothering to meet them. What should I do? Also, I sent an email to Just The Tip, but it's gone unanswered for over a week.

--Dry and Lonely

My shoulders tightened, and then I responded.

Dear Dry and Lonely,

Have you ever stopped to consider whether her needs were being met instead of focusing on your own? It doesn't sound like it to me. And honestly, the whole 'men have needs' bullshit is getting old. Women have needs too. We need to feel loved. Wanted. Important. Respected. Valued. Cared for.

Are you making her feel those things? If the answer is no or I don't know, then you need to try harder. If she isn't in the mood to have sex with you when you want it, then you need to step back and ask yourself why. Have you recently neglected her and what she needs? Did you present it as something fun you could do together, or did you demand that she get you off because you needed to feel good?

Figure out how to be less selfish, and maybe she'll come around. If not, be sure to send her over to Spill The Beans. I'll gladly treat her to a latte and discuss the new sex toys out there that can surely get her off so good she won't ever want anyone else to do the job for her.

I knew that part of my sour mood was from seeing Owen at La Salsa last night, but there was also something about this email that reminded me of Samuel and made my blood boil. That right there was the reason that I had never moved forward with any of my relationships and had sex with the guys. It was ridiculous how immature and arrogant most of them were.

I moved to the next email as I sipped a hot mug of coffee and curled my toes between the couch cushions.

Ask Mags,

I've made a mistake and lost the only girl I've ever felt something with. I was stupid and allowed my bruised ego to stand in the way. Now she won't talk to me, and I'm at a loss for what to do. I don't want to move on and forget about her. That would be like refusing to look up at the beautiful night sky because you'd missed seeing a shooting star as it passed by.

But I don't want to force her into anything, either. I respect her, and if she's really decided that she's moving on, then I won't try to stop her. But the problem is that I don't know how to tell the difference between her being pissed off at me and her being done with me. I can't just walk away and risk getting a second chance with her if she changes her mind.

Please tell me what to do. I'm so lost.

-- About to lose the greatest thing ever

My throat tightened as I read the email, feeling the heaviness of the emotions that were poured into his words. Tears stung my eyes as I quickly tried to blink them away. I set my coffee cup down and began typing.

Dear About to lose the greatest thing ever,

I can feel the pain you're feeling through your email and can empathize with you. I'm sorry that you're feeling this way.

Unfortunately, there are plenty of things that can cause tension in relationships, but it sounds like you've already realized what it was and are ready to fix it if you can. While I don't know what happened, I'm still rooting for you to get the second chance you're so desperately seeking.

I can't tell you what to do—only you can decide that. But I can tell you that actions always speak louder than words. You can talk until you're blue in the face, but your actions will be what she actually hears. Don't be afraid to step out of your comfort zone and show her what she needs to see.

Wishing you all the best. Please let me know how it goes.

I pressed send and wiped away the stray tear that had slipped down my face. Deciding that I'd had enough for the day, I shut off my laptop and put it on the table.

Leroy was pacing in his terrarium, looking ready to blast through the side of it, so I picked him up and set him down on the rug so he could roam around for a bit. While I tried to make Sundays my self-care days, I hadn't been up for anything today and decided that it was as good of a day as any to start some spring cleaning. Sure there was still a heavy layer of ice that covered my patio furniture outside, but one could be hopeful that it would be coming soon.

I started in the bathroom, cleaning everything until it sparkled, then moved on to my bedroom, which was already fairly clean given that I hardly spent any time in it other than to sleep. I opened the blinds to let in some light while I changed the sheets and made the bed. When I went to toss the dirty linens in the hamper, I'd found Leroy wedged between the washer and dryer, trying to pull a pair of panties out of the bottom.

The depths of my depression had brought me to the low of not bothering to care that he was eating more of my underwear. It seemed he had an obsession that even I couldn't cure him of.

I picked him up and set him back in the living room after closing the door to the laundry room to keep him out. I finished sweeping and was getting ready to start mopping the kitchen floor when I heard the doorbell.

"Who's here?" I asked Leroy, not that he could answer me. But that hadn't stopped me from talking to him nonstop since I'd gotten him.

As I pulled the door open, I heard a familiar squawk and smiled.

"Panty eater cocksucker." Pablo bounced excitedly, though it was the person whose shoulder he was bouncing on that surprised me the most.

"What are you doing here?" I asked, gripping the side of the door to keep my legs from betraying me and giving out.

"I'm sorry for showing up without an invite, but I really need to talk to you. Can I come in?"

Owen's eyes locked onto mine, and for a moment, it felt like we were the only two people left on the planet. That was until Pablo started cursing again and repeating some lyrics from an Eminem song.

"Please," he whispered.

"Please, Maggie. I'm so lonely. Lonely and horny. Horny and lonely. Pattthhheeetttiiiccc," Pablo sang.

My brow arched, wondering what exactly had been said in front of the bird.

"Okay." I pulled my shoulders back and moved aside to let them in.

"Turtle! Turtle food!" Pablo squawked, then flew off Owen's shoulder and landed on the coffee table, where he paced back and forth, watching Leroy.

"Is he going to try to eat him?" Owen asked with concern.

"No, he's fine." I laughed and let my shoulders relax a bit. "Ramona has been bringing Pablo over when she's stayed with me, and they get along just fine. He says turtle food because he likes to watch Leroy eat."

"Oh, okay." He closed the door behind him and shrugged off his jacket.

"Speaking of which, why do you have Pablo?" I asked, spinning around to face him. I hadn't anticipated how quickly he'd crossed the room until his hands gripped my hips to keep me from falling into him.

"Well, that was one of the things that I wanted to talk to you about."

I swallowed hard, feeling the tingle up my spine that I got when something terrible happened.

"Is Ramona okay? Did something happen?"

"No," Owen rushed out, his fingers still burning into my skin. "Ramona is fine."

I slowly blew out the breath I'd been holding and waited for him to continue.

"I have Pablo because I decided to adopt him."

My jaw dropped open as I looked from him to the bird that had hopped down onto the floor.

"What?"

He nodded and looked past me to the pets.

"Why would you do that?"

He smiled softly, his breathing calming me as I tried to figure out what was happening. Ramona loved Pablo and had just said last night that she wasn't going to adopt him out to anyone. Why the sudden change?

"I talked with Ramona and Dylan last night after you left La Salsa."

I wasn't sure if he'd seen me but should have known they would talk to him after I left.

"I asked for their help, and the next thing I knew, I was at Cool Cats, loading some ridiculously huge cage into Dylan's truck and bringing Pablo home with me."

"Okay," I paused. "I don't understand. Why did you take Pablo home? What's going on?" I could hear the panic and uncertainty in my voice, and I hated it.

"Because, Maggie, I needed something to show you that I'm not afraid of commitment. You said my actions would speak louder than words, so I wanted to show you that I could be what you wanted. I'm not sure if you know this or not, but African grey parrots have an extremely long lifespan—somewhere around sixty to eighty years. They are also highly social birds and rely on the stability of having one owner. That means that Pablo and I will be together for the rest of his life or mine—I'm not sure which of us is going to go first at this point."

He laughed nervously, and I could tell that this conversation still made him slightly uncomfortable, even though he was the one to bring it up.

"I've spent a lot of time online researching the best care to make sure I don't mess this up. I'm all in with Pablo and want to give him the best home I can."

"What about when you go back to New York?" I asked dumbly. I had plenty of questions, none of which were ready to come out yet.

"I have at least a year in Whiskey Mountain, maybe longer. After that, I'll talk to my office and discuss options." He shrugged.

"What does that mean?" I leaned closer, hanging on to his every word.

"It means that I've found a reason to stay in Whiskey Mountain, and there are a lot of small towns close by that I can work on developing."

"Pablo's one lucky bird," I said weakly when I felt Owen's hand gently touch my shoulder.

I wanted to give in and allow myself to fall into his embrace, but I couldn't.

"He is, but that's not why I'm considering staying here."

"No?" My voice was so quiet that I barely heard the words come out.

"Maggie, I know I messed up before, and I'm sorry. But I can't walk away from you, no matter how hard I try. There are a million reasons why this thing between us might not work, but I'm only looking for one reason for us to move forward and explore whatever this is. I'm not asking you to rush into anything with me, but I would love a second chance to pick up where things were going before."

I felt my cheeks flush as I remembered where we had left things before he walked out.

"I don't mean that exactly," he rushed to assure me. "I mean, I'm not saying I wouldn't enjoy doing it again, but I'm not pushing you to give me a second chance just so we can have sex. I wasn't lying when I said I would wait forever, Maggie. I will never force you to do anything you don't want."

My stomach felt swishy as my heart hammered against my chest. Was this really happening right now?

"I don't know, Owen," I sighed, taking a step back so I could get some fresh air that wasn't filled with the scent of his cologne. "What if it doesn't work out?"

"What if it does?"

I rubbed my lips together as my mind went a mile a minute. Deciding that I'd had enough thinking, I leaned forward and wrapped my arms around his neck before lifting my lips to his.

There was no hesitancy on his end as his mouth crashed over mine and parted, welcoming my tongue to explore.

Just like before, I felt my body come alive from his touch. Suddenly, I needed more. I pulled his head down, trying to get him closer to me even though we were already as close as we could get.

He reached down and lifted me to his hips before setting me down on the edge of the island. We kept kissing while his hands roamed over my back and grazed my butt.

Everything was alive and on fire as heat spread across my skin from his fingers.

I pulled away, panting for air, as he nudged my head to the side and kissed along my neck. I moaned helplessly as the warmth spread between my legs.

I knew it was a big step for Owen to adopt a bird and that he'd done that to show me that he wasn't afraid of commitment. When I'd gone back and forth in my head on the reasons to be with him versus the reasons we shouldn't be together, I couldn't help but focus on how I felt with him. It wasn't just that he was able to give me a mind-blowing orgasm with little effort, but now I realized that I felt safe and comfortable with him, as if I belonged in his arms.

His hands continued to roam along my back and sides but stayed away from the areas I wanted him to touch the most. I scooted closer and tried to rub myself against him, but he chuckled and pulled away.

My chest heaved as I watched him step back and study me before licking his lips. *Fuck, I was going to come just from watching him do that.*

"Maggie, Maggie, Maggie," he tsked, pulling his lip between his teeth.

"I want more," I panted, letting my legs slightly part.

His green eyes sparkled in the light as they danced with delight at how needy I'd suddenly become. Then he slowly rolled his sleeves up, one at a time, and I couldn't think of anything other than those strong hands touching my body and making me come again.

"I would love to give you more, Maggie, but I need something from you first."

My mind blanked as I thought about how I'd give him whatever he wanted right now. Blow job? Done. Keys to my house? You got it. Just make me come, and I'd do anything he'd ask.

"Okay," I whispered.

"I need you to tell me that you want to be with me and give this a chance. Not sex, Maggie, but be with me in a committed relationship. No other guys. No other girls. Just us."

"No sex?" I asked weakly.

"Not right away," he chuckled, then rubbed the side of his thumb gently across my cheek. "Trust me, we will wait until the right time. When you're ready."

"I'm ready," I offered excitedly.

"There's no rush, Maggie. I can make you feel plenty good without sex. But I need that commitment from you first. So, what do you say?"

I leaned back on my hands and pretended to think about it.

"Are you asking me to be your girlfriend?"

He nodded and gave me a panty-dropping smile.

"Okay," I shrugged, then giggled when he leaned in and tickled my sides until I squealed.

Twenty-Five
Owen

I stared at Maggie as she lay on the bed, her brown hair fanned out beneath her as her sparkling blue eyes watched me. The moment she'd agreed to be my girlfriend, I'd tossed her over my shoulder and carried her to the bedroom, ready to give her exactly what she'd been not so subtly asking for.

I did stop to ensure that Leroy and Pablo were fine, but Maggie smacked my ass and told me not to worry about them, so I didn't.

I stood in front of her, slowly undressing from the waist up as she focused on my every move. While I wanted nothing more than to be inside of her, I wasn't planning to do that until I knew for absolute certainty that she was ready. Whether that be tonight or a year from now, it didn't matter to me.

"You're killing me over here," she said as she rested against a pile of pillows.

"Eager are we?"

"A little," she giggled as her hand trailed up her thigh.

"Don't even think about it," I warned, nodding to her hand that was now hovering above her pussy. "I get to bring that orgasm out of you tonight."

"Well then, hurry up."

I tossed my shirt to the floor, then kicked off my jeans. Wearing just my briefs, I climbed beside her on the bed. She glanced down at the bulge and her face flushed.

"We're not rushing into anything tonight," I reminded her and brushed a strand of hair off her face.

"It's not like I haven't done other stuff," she said quietly. "I've done everything but sex. So, you know, I'm not a *total virgin*."

I nodded and leaned in, brushing my forehead against her cheek as I pushed her head to the side. I knew how much it turned her on when I kissed her neck, so I wanted to start there first.

A soft whimper escaped her lips as my tongue licked along her skin. She adjusted herself, allowing me more access as I trailed kisses down her collarbone and across her chest. My fingers skimmed along her thigh, slowly inching up toward her pussy.

Her chest rose and fell heavily as she panted while I pulled her t-shirt up and over her head. I was surprised that she wasn't wearing a bra underneath. My mouth eagerly moved across her breasts, pulling a hardened nipple and sucking it.

"Ohhh," she groaned and dug her nails into the sheets.

Focusing on how her body reacted to me, I laid my palm flat against her and gently rubbed the lace fabric over her slit. I could already feel how wet she was through the thin material and couldn't wait to feel her again as I slid it to the side and slipped a finger inside.

"Owen," she panted, bucking her hips off the bed.

I let go of one nipple, then pulled the other into my mouth and sucked hard while I eased another finger in. She was so fucking tight and wet that I felt like I was going to explode in my briefs. My erection strained against my stomach, and I shifted to give myself a little relief.

Knowing she was close to coming, I released her nipple and slid down her body, planting quick kisses over her abdomen before stopping at her pussy. I looked up to find her watching me as she bit her hand.

"Don't you dare keep those noises from me," I warned. "I want to hear every single sound you make, baby. You're about to come for me, and I want to hear it."

She nodded and dropped her hand as I hooked the thin straps of her thong under my thumbs and removed them. Tossing them aside, I licked my lips and got an up-close look at her beautiful pussy dripping with need. Locking eyes with her again, I lowered my head between her legs and licked.

A sharp exhale filled the air around us as her head fell back against the pillows. I smiled and continued to torture her with my tongue as I flicked her clit before taking it into my mouth and sucking while my fingers continued to fuck her.

"Fuuuccckkk," she cried out, pressing her thighs together as her orgasm crashed over her.

I kept my pace and waited until I felt the last spasm before I let go. I slowly rolled off her and wiped my mouth, loving how she looked post-orgasm.

"That was amazing," she sighed, rolling over to look at me. "But as your *girlfriend*, I'm entitled to take care of *that*." She nodded to the rock-hard erection in my briefs.

"We don't need to worry about that right now," I said softly. The last thing that I wanted was for her to feel like sex stuff was obligatory. If I made her come, it was because I wanted to. Not because I expected something in return.

"Oh please," she laughed and rolled over, her hand squeezing my dick. "I know you don't think you're going to come in here, sporting the biggest hard-on I've ever seen and not let me play with it."

A cocky grin spread across my face.

"You don't have to," I assured her.

"I know. I want to."

She squeezed closer to me, and I wrapped my arm around her shoulders as I laid on my back and allowed her hands to roam over my briefs. Her every touch felt amazing, but I was about to come if she didn't stop soon. As if sensing my need, she stopped and pulled my briefs down, allowing my cock to spring free.

Tossing them to the side, she grabbed me between her hands and slowly stroked me.

I let out a hiss between my teeth and found myself gripping the back of her head as she lowered her mouth and took me inside of it.

"Maggie," I moaned helplessly.

I wanted to tell her to stop, that she didn't owe me anything, but the way she worked her tongue and teeth over me told me that she wanted to do this. Not only that, she wasn't lying about having done it before.

Her hands worked the length that didn't fit in her mouth, even after I'd touched the back of her throat. On occasion, she'd reach back and caress my balls, sending me nearly over the edge. I was going to come soon at this rate.

She sucked harder and faster, forcing my balls to tighten beneath me.

"Maggie," I warned. "I'm going to come."

She locked even tighter around me and kept going until I exploded and shot ropes of cum down her throat.

Once my body stopped jerking, she slowly pulled away and wiped her mouth.

I panted as I tried to think of something to say, but when

she laid down and cuddled next to me, I didn't bother. Her fingers curled into the hair on my chest while I held her, and for once, everything felt like it was perfect.

Twenty-Six
Maggie

"It's been two weeks, and you guys still haven't had sex?" Ramona asked in disbelief as she sat across from me at Spill The Beans. We'd already closed for the day, but she hung around for a cup of coffee and to catch up on girl talk.

"He said he's waiting until he knows I'm ready."

"Have you told him that you are? Hell, I'm getting blue balls from waiting this long," she joked and sipped her latte.

"I've told him, but it's usually when we're already doing other stuff, so I don't think he trusts it. I think he thinks that I'm just lost in the moment and that I'll regret it later."

"That's way too much thinking." She wrinkled her nose.

"Tell me about it."

"So do something to show him that's not the case."

"Like what?" I sipped mine and then took a bite of the apple crumble muffin I'd saved for myself this morning.

"You guys have another date tonight, right?"

"Yeah."

"Your place or his?"

"Mine."

"Okay, so put on some of your sluttiest lingerie and then

surprise him with it as soon as he gets there. That way, you can let him know you're ready before anything happens."

"I can't do that," I said sadly. My shoulders slumped with disappointment.

"Why not?" She frowned.

"Because Leroy ate my last pair of sexy undies."

"What is it with that damn turtle and underwear?"

"I have no idea. But I'm officially out of sexy ones."

Ramona's phone dinged with a new text message, so I popped another bite of muffin into my mouth and waited for her to be done. She was grinning ear to ear, and I knew she must be talking to a new guy. So much for waiting a while before moving on from Daniel.

"Where were we?" she asked, then her brows rose when she remembered. "Oh yeah, what about the new ones you just bought?"

"He ate those too."

"How? Haven't you learned not to leave them on the floor?"

I laughed and felt the blush spread across my cheeks.

"Yeah, but it wasn't my fault. Owen came over and started kissing me, and I forgot that they were in the basket of clothes I was working on putting away when he got there. Leroy took advantage of pulling them out of the pile while Owen and I were in the bathroom."

"Bathroom?" She raised her brows and wiggled them.

"He had been out for a run and passed by my house to say hi. I offered to make him dinner, and he said he wanted to clean up first. One thing led to another, and he went down on me in the shower."

"You dirty, dirty girl."

"Actually, I was the clean one," I giggled.

"Okay, then let's go buy you some new lingerie for tonight." She got up and gave me a pointed look while she waited for me.

Two hours and fifty different outfits later, I was standing in front of the full-length mirror in my bedroom, regretting my choice.

Ramona and the sales lady convinced me this would look hot and make Owen crazy, so I got it. Now I couldn't help but feel nervous and insecure as I stared at the see-through black lace that barely covered my breasts and the matching thong that rode up my ass.

Before I could change my mind, the doorbell rang. I tossed on the robe that I'd bought to go with it and padded down the hallway to the door.

Leroy was secured in his terrarium, away from the bag of other lingerie I'd decided to purchase as well. I had washed the set for tonight but hadn't bothered with the others yet.

I opened the door and took him in as he held out a dozen roses to me.

"Thank you," I said softly, taking them from him and smelling them. "They're beautiful."

"You're beautiful." He leaned in and kissed my cheek.

I waited for him to come in before I closed the door and locked it. My palms started to feel sweaty as the realization of what I was about to do hit me.

"So," I said nervously. "I have something I want to show you."

"Oh yeah?" His crooked brow still did something to me.

I ignored the heat spreading between my legs and forced my fingers to work the tie on my robe. Once it was undone, I slowly opened it, trying to look sexier than I felt as I stood before him in the skimpy lingerie.

His Adam's apple bobbed in his throat as he swallowed. I felt the heat of his gaze as his eyes traveled over my body, taking in every single inch.

"I like it," he said, his voice gruff.

"Tonight is the night," I replied steadily.

"Okay." He took two steps and was right in front of me as his fingers trailed over the thin lace of the bra.

"Okay?" I couldn't believe he was finally agreeing to give me what I wanted.

"If you feel like you're ready, we can have sex."

"I'm ready. Now. Right now." I nodded to the bedroom. "I've already ordered a pizza, so we don't have to worry about dinner. We can eat when we're done. I also tipped them twenty dollars to just leave it on the doorstep and not bother us with ringing the doorbell."

I watched as he struggled to fight back his laughter.

"I don't want anything to get in the way of this happening," I added.

"Noted."

"Okay," I breathed out. The only problem was that now I didn't know what to do with myself.

"Would you like me to take over?" he asked as he rocked back on his heels and shoved his hands in his pockets.

I nodded, suddenly worrying that maybe I'd bitten off more than I could chew.

As if noticing my discomfort—which was blatantly

obvious—he reached out and gently stroked my cheek.

"Relax, baby. You're still in control, and nothing will happen if you don't want it to."

"Okay."

He pulled me close and wrapped his arms around my waist as his lips brushed against mine. And just like that, all of my worries melted away.

Once I knew that Owen wasn't going to talk me out of having sex with him, my nerves settled, and I was able to relax. We moved into the bedroom and made out for a while before he went down on me and gave me another mind-blowing orgasm.

I reached over to stroke him, but he gently pushed my hand away and held it.

"Do you still want to?" he asked softly, kissing behind my ear.

"Yes," I replied quickly. "I want to have sex with you, Owen."

A low growl slipped through his lips as he rolled over and pinned me to the bed.

"If at any time you want to stop, I need you to tell me. There's nothing wrong with not going all the way, okay?"

I nodded.

"And if it hurts, you have to tell me that as well. You're going to be super tight, and I might stretch you. But I don't want this to be painful, so I need you to be honest and let me know if it is."

I nodded again, wondering just how bad it was going to hurt.

Owen lifted his hips and pulled his briefs off, allowing the beast to spring free. Then he grabbed a condom from the dresser and rolled it over his length. I watched everything as it happened, trying to soak in every detail.

He rolled on top of me and lowered his mouth to mine as he slowly kissed me.

"We can stop at any time," he whispered.

My legs parted, allowing him access while he shifted and lined himself up at my entrance.

"Are you ready?"

I held my breath as I nodded.

"Say it, Maggie."

"I'm ready."

"Good girl," he whispered, then gently pushed inside.

I gasped at the intrusion, feeling a slight sting as his thick cock pushed through. He stopped and waited for me to adjust to him before inching in. It was the slowest motion, and the stinging stopped almost as quickly as it started.

I could see him struggling to control himself as he hovered above me. Once he was fully seated, I reached up and caressed his jaw. His arms looked huge as they flexed beside me, showing off the tattoos that I'd come to admire.

Gently, I rocked my hips to let him know that I was ready for more. He scrunched his face and bit down on his lip as I squeezed his cock with my pussy.

"Give me more, Owen," I coaxed. I couldn't imagine that anything else was going to be painful, and didn't want him to keep treating me like I was some delicate flower he was about to break.

His eyes searched mine, and then he nodded as he rocked into me, pushing himself even deeper.

"Ahhh," I cried out, scratching my nails down his back. He pumped faster, and soon we found a rhythm as our bodies moved against each other. My body felt wonderfully filled as he reached down and started to rub my clit.

My legs quivered as they fell to the sides to allow him complete access to my body. He lifted himself back and rested on his knees while keeping his cock still inside of me. His thumb caressed the heightened bundle of nerves as he watched his dick slide slowly in and out of me.

"This is perfection," he commented proudly. "Such perfection."

I could feel my orgasm building as he continued to rub faster and right as I was about to come, he slammed into me, sending a jolt of pleasure through me as I cried out his name. He kept pounding, not too hard but hard enough that I could hear the sound of his balls clapping against my ass. Then I felt him tighten above me as he shuddered and unloaded into the condom.

Once he was done, he pulled back slightly and studied my face to make sure I was okay.

"That was incredible," I assured him, gently stroking his cheek. "I can't wait to do it again."

"You're going to be the death of me," he chuckled, then laid his forehead against mine.

While I'd waited a long time to lose my virginity, I couldn't imagine waiting another second before I could feel Owen inside of me again.

Epilogue
Maggie

Three Months Later

"You're going to get a sunburn," Owen said as his shadow cast over me. I shielded my eyes with my hand and looked up to find him standing there with a bottle of sunscreen.

"Sit up, and I'll put some on you."

"Like you did with the massage oil the other night?" I teased but did as he asked.

It was unusually hot for May, and I'd decided to spend some time sunbathing in the backyard while Leroy got some sun. Except when I found out that Owen was coming home early from work today, I'd decided to go topless and wear my skimpiest bikini bottoms.

"I didn't hear any complaints after I massaged you. If anything, those moans begged me for more."

That was true, I had begged. But that wasn't unusual. It was like having sex with Owen unlocked some mysterious sex-fiend I couldn't contain when he was around. And now that he'd decided to take a permanent position in Whiskey Mountain, he was at my house often. So much so that I'd convinced him to move in with me and give up the rental home they'd initially put him in. There was more space at my place, so we spent most of our time there anyway.

"I would never complain about a massage. I just wasn't aware of the dick method."

"Well, my hands were a little busy with your shoulders, so it decided to jump in and get those hard-to-reach spots." He leaned close and whispered in my ear, "like your g-spot."

I had learned a lot about myself and what I liked in bed over the past three months, including that the g-spot very much existed and that some women are natural squirters. Ramona was now obsessed with learning as much as she could about it and was determined to find a guy who could do it for her.

"Feel free to massage that anytime you'd like," I offered, rolling over onto my back.

He stepped back and stared at my bare breasts as he squirted more lotion into the palm of his hand. I expected him to bend down and rub it on the same way he'd done my back, but instead, he kneeled beside me and slowly dripped it onto my body as if it were hot wax—which we had recently experimented with as well.

"I'll be massaging it here in a minute," he muttered, then spread the lotion across me, slowly focusing on my nipples as he traced circles around them.

"We don't have time; Ramona and Dylan will be here in half an hour."

"They can watch."

"I'm sure Ramona would," I laughed. "But I don't think I'm willing to listen to her obsess over your huge cock once she sees it."

"Fine," he sighed. "But in that case, you'd better put on more clothes before they get here."

He stood up and rubbed his hands together.

"Alright. I was just about cooked anyway."

He reached out a hand and helped me up. I wrapped my arms around his neck and pulled him into me for a kiss. Even after endless amounts of dirty, kinky sex, nothing made me feel better than the innocent kisses we shared together.

There was a lot of chemistry between us, but there was also this deep connection that neither of us had ever felt with anyone before. For the longest time, I'd been so afraid that I wouldn't find true love that I almost missed it when it was right in front of me the entire time.

****

Thank you for reading Maggie and Owen's story! Can't get enough of them? I have a bonus epilogue for you!

https://dl.bookfunnel.com/zvj33o4tx2

If you're looking for more Whiskey Mountain romance, Ramona will be getting her story in Something To Think About. You can preorder your copy here:

https://books2read.com/u/3GWAan

Other Books By Samantha Baca

The Haven Brook Series
(small town romantic suspense):

'Til Death Do Us Part (Haven Brook Book 1)

https://books2read.com/u/m2RJNR

The Cradle Will Fall (Haven Brook Book 2)

https://books2read.com/u/b6O0QE

The Ties That Bind (Haven Brook Book 3)

https://books2read.com/u/mqgoz8

A Very Haven Christmas (Haven Brook Book 4- Novella)

https://books2read.com/u/mvqGjj

Three Strikes, You're Gone (Haven Brook Book 5)

https://books2read.com/u/mvqL2z

__The Dark Shadows Series (romantic suspense)__

Five Steps Ahead (Dark Shadows Book 1)

https://books2read.com/u/38Q0gO

Ten Seconds Too Late (Dark Shadows Book 2)

https://books2read.com/u/3JRgVB

Against The Clock (Dark Shadows Book 3)

https://books2read.com/u/m2YwoR

Out Of Time (Dark Shadows Book 4)

https://books2read.com/u/4DKMoP

__The Stone Creek Series (small town- novellas)__

Chocolate Covered Mistletoe (Stone Creek Book 1)

https://books2read.com/u/3LRk9N

Candy Coated Promises (Stone Creek Book 2)

https://books2read.com/u/mldP5Y

Pumpkin Spiced Possibilities (Stone Creek Book 3)

https://books2read.com/u/bojdwV

<u>Beaumont Creek Series (small town)</u>

Just One Time (Beaumont Creek Book 1)

https://books2read.com/u/3G52zK

Second Chances (Beaumont Creek Book 2)

https://books2read.com/u/4Aj6Z0

Third Time's The Charm (Beaumont Creek Book 3)

https://books2read.com/u/b5lEyG

Four-ever Single (Beaumont Creek Book 4)

Preorder link coming soon

Fifth Wheel (Beaumont Creek Book 5)

Preorder link coming soon

<u>Whiskey Mountain Series (small town- novellas)</u>

Something To Talk About

https://books2read.com/u/4X62ag

Something To Think About

https://books2read.com/u/3GWAan

Something To Believe In

https://books2read.com/u/3yVzgB

Something To Live For

Preorder link coming soon

<u>Standalone Books</u>

One Last Wish

https://books2read.com/u/mqg7D9

Finding Love In Apartment 2C (novella)

https://books2read.com/u/bze9aZ

Cocky Counsel: A Hero Club Novel

https://books2read.com/u/31Kzkn

All Is Fair In Food And War (novella)

https://books2read.com/u/bp8qjX

<u>Holiday Books (novellas)</u>

Snow Place To Go

https://books2read.com/u/4A560N

A Christmas Wish

https://books2read.com/u/4EKXpE

Blame It On The Mistletoe

https://books2read.com/u/bw1rqe

Holiday Hijinks

https://books2read.com/u/4DP6Ze

Acknowledgments

If someone would have told me five years ago that I would write and publish ONE book, I would have thought they were crazy. Now here we are, almost 3 years after I not only published my first book, but I've also completed eighteen others! It blows my mind that I am literally living my dream.

So much of that is due to the wonderful readers who have given my books a chance and fallen in love with the characters that I've written. I've met so many beautiful friends along the way and some have turned into alpha and beta readers, while some gobble up every book I write, as soon as it comes out.

I couldn't do any of this without the support of my family, friends, editing team, and everyone else who has cheered me on along the way. Thank you so much to everyone for their continuous help, it means the world to me.

Niki, you've been such an amazing friend and alpha reader, I can't imagine what this story would have been like without your help.

Azucena and Chelsea, it's crazy to think we've done this many books together, isn't it? Thank you for sticking with me!

Amanda, Adrianna, Katy, and Nicole, thank you for taking the time to beta read this for me and give me your feedback! You're the best!

Richard, sometimes I think you like me writing books just so I can gush over how amazing you are in the acknowledgements. But then again, you know that I would stand at the top of a mountain and shout how much I love and adore you for everyone to hear. You're one of the best things that has ever happened to me and I love you so much. Thank you for everything you do.

To my girls—you are amazing and wonderful just the way you are. Don't ever change. And no, you can't read the books I write for a quite a few years… and even then, we'll have to talk first.

If you've taken the time to read every single word I've written, I would love if you wouldn't mind jumping online and leaving a quick review to let me know what you thought! Thank you for being an amazing reader, but most importantly—thank you for being you.

About the Author

Samantha lives in the southwest with her husband and two small children after abandoning her childhood dream of living in a cabin in Colorado when she found that she couldn't afford to live there and was deathly allergic to the woods. When she's not writing, she's usually spouting off sarcastic remarks while drinking wine out of a coffee mug to look like a functional adult while chasing down her toddlers. She enjoys spending time with her family, watching reruns of Friends, and the 24/7 flow of coffee that can be found in her veins. Be sure to follow her on social media for updates on what she's working on.

You can find her here:

Facebook: https://www.facebook.com/AuthorSamanthaBaca

Instagram: https://instagram.com/author_samantha_baca

Goodreads: http://www.goodreads.com/authorsamanthabaca

Facebook Reader Group:

https://www.facebook.com/groups/2945710968775398/

Webpage: https://authorsamanthabaca.wordpress.com

Newsletter: http://eepurl.com/g0NcSj

www.ingramcontent.com/pod-product-compliance
Lightning Source LLC
Chambersburg PA
CBHW061538310726
48972CB00008B/2508